D0793178

BOOK 2:

THE BLUE PLANETS WORLD

SIRENS

BY

DARCY PATTISON

Mims House, Little Rock, AR

Copyright © 2017 by Darcy Pattison.
All rights reserved. No part of this publication may be repro-
duced, distributed or transmitted in any form or by any means,
including photocopying, recording, or other electronic or mechan-
ical methods, without the prior written permission of the publisher, except in the case of brief quotations embodied in critical
reviews and certain other noncommercial uses permitted by copyright law.

Mims House
1309 Broadway
Little Rock, AR 72202
www.mimshouse.com

Publisher's Note: This is a work of fiction. Names, characters, places,
and incidents are a product of the author's imagination. Locales and
public names are sometimes used for atmospheric purposes. Any re-
semblance to actual people, living or dead, or to businesses, compa-
nies, events, institutions, or locales is completely coincidental.

Publisher's Cataloging-in-Publication data

Names: Pattison, Darcy, author.
Title: Sirens / by Darcy Pattison.
Series: The Blue Planets World.
Description: Description: Little Rock, AR: Mims House, 2017.
Identifiers: ISBN 978-1-62944-081-1 (Hardcover) | 978-1-62944-080-4
(pbk.) | 978-1-62944-079-8 (ebook)
Summary: Aliens beg refuge on Earth. The Phoke, Mer people, are
forced to come out of hiding and take a place at the negotiation table.
Subjects: LCSH Extraterrestrial beings--Fiction. | Mermaids and
mermen--Fiction. | Parent and child--Fiction. | Adoption--Fiction. |
Racially mixed families--Fiction. | Refugees--Fiction. | Science fic-
tion. | BISAC JUVENILE FICTION / Science Fiction
Classification: LCC PZ7.P27816 Si 2017 | DDC [Fic]--dc23

Printed in the United States of America

Other Novels by Darcy Pattison

The Blue Planets World
Envoys, Prequel
Sleepers, Book 1
Sirens, Book 2
Pilgrims, Book 3

Liberty
Longing for Normal
Vagabonds
The Girl, the Gypsy and the Gargoyle
The Wayfinder

THE DEPTHS

December 10

Em Tullis stared straight into the eyes of her family doctor, Dr. Max Bari. She was groggy and still sick, but she knew who he was. How did she get here, though? Where was *here*?

Weakly, she lifted a hand. Thick glass separated her from Dr. Bari. Was she in an isolation chamber?

"Hurry!" Dr. Bari called to someone behind him. Through the thick glass, the words were muffled. "She's waking up, and I can't give her anything else."

Behind Dr. Bari's head, dark clouds scudded across a pale gray sky. Yet Em felt warm, calm.

"Get that pod in the water!" Dr. Bari called.

Pod?

His face disappeared, and then her world tilted. Em realized that she was strapped down to some sort of bed. She wore a loose-fitting shirt and pants. The container that held her—a pod?—was almost upright now, and there was a flash of blue-gray. Sky?

Suddenly, the pod dropped, like she was at the top of a roller coaster and was now plunging downward. With a jolt, the pod slammed into something hard, then jerked back upward. Em squeezed her eyes shut, expecting to—what? To die, or to be hurt, or—she didn't know. Her pod bobbed up and down for a few seconds until it slowed, and then it pitched into a horizontal position.

She was still alive.

Em opened her eyes. Her pod was face down in water, and straps kept her in place. Dr. Bari hovered underneath, staring up at her. Yes, it was him. The last time she'd seen him was in her parents' house. She'd been sick, dizzy. She had walked downstairs to tell Mom that she was feeling worse, and Dr. Bari was there, sitting on her couch, talking to Mom and Dad. She only caught a few words.

"It's spelled P-h-o-k-e. You say it, Fo-key."

"And Em is a Phoke?" Mom asked.

Em must've made a sound because Dad whirled around to see her standing on the stairs. She was dizzy, and badly in need of a bath and a mouth wash for bad breath. Dad scooped her up, letting her face snuggle into the rough stubble on his neck. She shivered, but Dad murmured soothingly, "It's okay."

He carried her back to her bed upstairs and tucked her in.

After Dad left, Em hauled herself out of bed, found Dr. Bari's business card from the hospital sitting on her desk, scrawled a note to Jake and left it under the photo she'd taken when he wasn't looking. Would he find it?

No, she thought as she drifted back to the present. The question she needed to know was what body of water was she in? Puget Sound? Pacific Ocean? And why was she here? What was Phoke?

But she was too sick—or too drugged—to react quickly.

Dr. Bari gave her a thumbs up and disappeared.

Groggily, she thought, *something is odd about Dr. Bari.*

She felt her pod rotating, and then the sky reappeared, bobbing up and down. Waves. Then, it was a place with strong waves. Probably not Puget Sound.

There came a roar. Vibrations shuddered through her pod. A motor.

Her pod tilted again, pointing her feet deeper into the water. The light from the sky slowly faded, and her feet sank into darkness. Her pod was diving, some motor pushing it deeper and deeper.

Terror gripped her, and Em clutched the fabric sheets upon which she lay. She tried to pull herself to the right to align her body better in the center of the pod, feeling unreasonably that if she could straighten herself, this would all go away. But the straps held her fast; she couldn't budge.

Above her a fish flashed past, and then a jellyfish. They were going too fast to tell more than that. But it must be an ocean. Lakes would be much more shallow.

Where was Dr. Bari taking her? He was supposed to be medically treating her fainting and weakness, some weird kind of illness. But this sure wasn't an ambulance.

She blinked. In the distance now was a faint glow. As she watched, the light grew brighter. How was that possible in the depths of the ocean? Then a dark hulk—an underwater mountain—resolved into—no, it couldn't be. A building. A secret underwater compound? A military installation? What? She wanted to pound on the pod, to demand that Dr. Bari explain what was happening but her hands couldn't escape the bands that held her down.

Then it hit her. She had stared straight into Dr. Bari's eyes. He wasn't wearing a scuba mask. Or a tank. Or carrying any air. That meant—

Em squeezed her eyes shut. Dr. Bari didn't need scuba to breath underwater. That meant he must be a Risonian, a Shark. She'd been kidnapped by aliens.

A SPLASH OF COLD WATER

December 17

Jake Rose stared at the massive metal struts of the red bridge above him, amazed again at the contradictions presented by humans. They knew how to turn practical things into things of beauty, but not how to stop species from going extinct.

David Gordon gestured to a couple cars that had stopped near them. Poking out the windows were long camera lenses. "And did you have to bring the *paparazzi*?"

They were just outside Edinburgh, visiting the Scotland National Aquarium. It was Jake's first "official" visit as the Risonian ambassador's son, and it looked like the photographers would follow them everywhere for a while. He shouldn't be surprised. Rison was a planet half-a-galaxy away, the first extraterrestrial contact Earth had ever made. Rison's planetary core was dangerously unstable, and his mother was trying to negotiate a place on Earth for Risonians to immigrate. Everything he did or didn't do was under constant scrutiny.

Reading from a guidebook, Jillian Lusk said, "The Forth Rail Bridge was built in 1890 and is the second longest cantilevered bridge in the world." She pulled out her cell phone and started snapping photos. Her white-blond hair almost gave her a Nordic look. Here on the North Sea, people often guessed she was Swedish or Norwegian. At 5'11", she was tall for a high school Freshman.

"Let me see that," David demanded.

She dodged him, so he grabbed her shoulders. Tall and lanky, he was a head taller than Jillian, so he could see over her shoulder. She pointed to the bridge's photo in the book. Then, spinning, she put the book in her purse, and ordered, "Stand over here. Let me get your pictures."

Jake and David dutifully followed orders.

As Jillian clicked away—she liked a different photo for each of her social media accounts—David said sideways to Jake, "Is she going to be a tour guide and selfie freak all week?"

Jake just shrugged. Although the boys didn't see eye-to-eye, Jake had just hit six feet tall. When they finally got back to Bainbridge Island, he planned to hit the hoops so he could try out for the basketball team. If that failed, he'd join David on the sculling team.

Jillian sighed and waved at her phone, "Jake, do you ever smile? Every picture I take of you has a frown."

Jake put on a fake grin, flashing his teeth for a moment. "There."

Jillian looked up from the phone. "I missed it. Of course."

A brisk wind blew across Firth of Forth, and Jake turned back to the embassy limo for a jacket. Colonel Lett was already holding it out. Mom had insisted that Jake come along to Edinburgh for a mini-summit with European leaders and more political negotiations, but they'd brought several bodyguards. Today, Mom had needed Colonel Barbena, a female bodyguard for a women's luncheon. She could pass for a human female, albeit a tall one at 5'10'. Although you never saw Colonel Lett wearing anything but military fatigues or uniforms, Colonel Barbena could wear stylish Earth fashions and blend in with a crowd.

That meant Colonel Lett, who was usually assigned to Mom, was given orders to protect Jake instead.

Jake sighed. "Are you sure we have to spend a whole hour in here? Can't we do something else?"

"You know your duty," Lett said curtly. "You can't ignore it."

This was why Jake wasn't pleased when they were assigned Colonel Lett for the day. With him, it was always about duty.

Of course, Jake knew he couldn't shirk his duty. But the responsibilities of being the Face of Rison felt wrong. It was like putting on a mask that perpetually smiled. He hated how it felt so artificial, so forced. His mom expected his help in convincing Earth's politicians to give asylum to Risonians. But he was no politician. All he could do was smile for a camera. And apparently, Jillian didn't think he did that very well, either.

He briefly turned on his cell phone to stare at the screensaver photo. Em. Dark hair, dark eyes. He sucked in a breath of frustration. He wanted to concentrate on finding his girlfriend, who had been missing for three weeks. Em had been hospitalized with a mysterious illness, and when she went home from the hospital, she simply disappeared. Her parents were gone, her sister was gone, and Em was gone. He'd found her doctor's business card with two words scrawled on it: "Phoke. Help!" No one knew what it meant. After an Internet search, the only place he saw the word Phoke used was in Scotland.

Jake had convinced Mom that the teenage Face of Rison needed to be seen with human teens, so David and Jillian had been invited on the Edinburgh trip. Of course, they weren't human; they were Risonian also, part of an advance group of Risonians who had lived on Earth for over a decade. Since they'd grown up on Earth, they knew almost nothing about Rison. That meant their behavior was like that of any American teen, and they'd be good cover. And because they weren't human, Jake wouldn't have to be on his guard all the time.

Most importantly, though, his friends could help him locate Em. If only he didn't have these official duties.

Jake strode resolutely toward the aquarium that lay under the massive bridge. Better to get this over with.

"Good morning." A red-cheeked blond lady with curly hair and blue eyes met them at the door. "My name is Enid Ways, and this is Fairfax Lyme. We're your guides for the day."

Since Christmas was this week, green holly wreaths with bright red berries hung on every door.

The man beside Enid, probably of Indian descent with his warm brown skin, wore a Deep Sea World navy shirt and khaki pants. "We're honored to have you here," he said. "Earth's oceans must be fascinating for you."

Enid took over the tour guide role saying, "We have a number of exhibits that might interest you, including the Underwater Safari, a tunnel that goes under and through a water tank. But we thought you might like to go behind the scenes first and meet Priscilla."

Jillian said, "Priscilla who?"

"I know," David said with a quick smile. "I've been reading the Edinburgh newspapers online. You've got an octopus."

Fairfax nodded at David, a gesture of approval. "Not just any octopus," Fairfax said. "A wee little, wayward octopus."

"Exactly," Enid said with a tinkling laugh. "She's been a handful."

Jake raised an eyebrow, so Fairfax launched into a story.

"She's pure dead brilliant, she is, at escaping. Seven times, she's climbed out of her tank. Octopuses are hard to keep caged. Outside the water tank, they can walk—after a fashion—and can hide in tight spots that make them hard to reach."

"Can't you just grab a tentacle and pull them out?" Jillian asked.

"First, it's not tentacles," Enid said. "A tentacle only has one sucker and octopus arms have suckers along the whole length."

"And no," Fairfax said. "Each sucker might have 500 pounds of force, and they have over 1000 suckers. You'd never just grab an octopus's arm and hope to pull her out of anything."

Wistfully, Jake thought, Em would have loved this. Anything about the ocean fascinated her.

Enid led the way into a spacious but dimly lit room. Before them were three square water tanks, each about four feet tall. Made of thick, clear glass, they were accessed by a two-step set of wide stairs on each side.

The top glass of the tank was hinged about three feet back. Fairfax on one side and Enid on the other, they folded back the top. Then, Enid knelt on the top step and slapped the water lightly.

Something deep in the water flashed, and suddenly an octopus pressed against the glass right in front of them. The air smelled salty and fishy, a comforting smell to Jake. And the octopus absolutely captured his attention.

Priscilla was a curled octopus, Enid explained, common in the north Atlantic and North Sea. They were fairly small, maybe twenty inches long. Rusty red with white spots, her body and legs were exquisitely proportioned. Jake had assumed an octopus's legs just dangled. Instead, she had hers tucked up under her body. She looked like a polite old lady with her hands folded in her lap.

Suddenly, Priscilla rose until her eyes were above the water, and she stared at her visitors. Her dark eyes scanned Jake up and down.

Jake shivered in delight. She was amazing.

"She's quite intelligent," Enid said, "and she knows each of her caregivers really well." She pulled off her t-shirt, revealing a waterproof vest, and then plunged her hands into the water. "Her tank is really cold because she normally lives over 50 meters deep. For you Yanks, that's over 150 feet deep."

Fascinated, Jake watched as Priscilla's arms reached for Enid and encircled her, suckers gently undulating like the octopus was licking her—or tasting her. Just watching made his own arms tingle.

Enid nodded to Jake, Jillian, and David. "Would you like to meet her?"

Eagerly, Jake said, "Yes!"

On a table beside the tank was a stack of white towels and waterproof vests. Fairfax gestured toward them and said, "Choose one that fits and the bathroom makes a good changing room." He waved toward marked bathrooms on the far wall. They quickly changed and came out a bit self-conscious.

Excitement made Jake walk on tiptoe, as if afraid to break the spell that Priscilla had cast on everyone. Swimming in the Risonian seas, he'd seen many strange and wonderful creatures. Compared to them, Priscilla was equally beautiful, but more intriguing. He stopped at the tank and stared at the octopus who was still playing with Enid. He splashed a finger in the water, but Priscilla ignored him. Maybe his wonder came from the octopus's ability to choose whether she would be concerned with his fingers. It was more than instinct; there was an intelligence in her eyes.

He laughed awkwardly. "What if she doesn't like aliens?" Suddenly, it mattered whether she liked him or not. Risonians needed to be comfortable in Earth's waters, and that meant co-existing peacefully with most marine life.

Enid raised an eyebrow and said, "Only one way to find out."

Jake stared at the oddly shaped octopus. Humans and Risonians had a head, a body, and then arms and legs. The octopus had a body and a head, and arms came last. That was a more alien body structure than Risonian anatomy.

He knelt on the top step beside the tank, took a deep breath and plunged his hands into the water. Deliberately, he flapped his hands in the "friend" signal that he would've used with sea creatures back on Rison. He'd also used it with sharks in the Gulf of Mexico, and they roughly understood, so it might work here, too.

One of Priscilla's arms unwound from Enid. The tip reached for him, moving delicately, cautiously.

Jake held rigid and allowed Priscilla's arm to touch his forearm. The tip suddenly flattened and the octopus's arm lay flat across his entire forearm. The suckers rippled, tickling Jake till he almost threw her off. But then, another octopus arm and another stretched for him. Three arms embraced both forearms. Jake had the absurd thought that it was three arms against two now.

Or maybe it wasn't so absurd. The gentle pressure on his arms increased until Jake struggled to keep his balance. She was a small octopus, but he was forced to squat lower, letting his arms stay in the tank, but allowing him to lean against the tank wall and resist the pull.

She pulled harder.

"Hey, there," he said in what he hoped was a friendly voice.

Priscilla's body was out of the water now, and her eyes stared straight into his. The water around his arms shook with a sudden vibration, as if the octopus was answering his "Friend" question. And then, she jerked him forward.

Jake braced himself harder, his heart beating faster in sudden fear. How strong was this octopus? He didn't notice individual suckers. Rather, his whole arm throbbed as the suckers continually adjusted and retightened.

Alarmed, Enid cried, "Is she pulling you in?"

Through gritted teeth, Jake said, "She's trying."

Enid and Fairfax were beside him immediately, gently inserting their own arms beneath his and taking some pressure off.

Suddenly, Priscilla withdrew all her arms and fell back under the surface, squirting away to a rock, where Jake watched in fascination as she rapidly camouflaged herself. If he hadn't known where she had gone, Jake would swear that was a rock, not an octopus. He'd never seen such complete camouflage. What a strange, incredible creature!

Amazed, he stood, turned to Enid. and said, "Wow."

From the corner of his eye, he caught movement; Priscilla was back in front of him and suddenly, she squirted him in the face with a cold stream of water.

Dumfounded, Jake froze in place.

But Priscilla was in movement. She squirted David's face, and then Jillian's, both of them gasping at the shock of bitterly cold water. Quickly, Priscilla returned to her rock, and camouflaged herself until it seemed she had disappeared, and the tank was empty.

Enid and Fairfax stared at them with stunned expressions.

David broke the tension—he was always the peacemaker—by laughing, a terrific howl that made the others gape. He pointed at Jake and managed to gasp out, "Priscilla doesn't like you!"

Jake wiped water from his face and grinned back. "Or you."

"Aw," Jillian said. "I wanted to formally meet her."

Nervously, Enid and Fairfax smiled, too. "Maybe that's not a good idea, since she's upset."

Jake grabbed a towel from the table, and soberly started drying his face. He didn't like this at all. Why had Priscilla squirted him? Did she really understand that he was alien? And had she really sent vibrations that said, "Dangerous"?

Jillian, of course, insisted on a selfie photo of the three of them sitting on the water tank's steps so they could see the water in the background. "Put on your smile, Jake," she warned.

Obediently, he contorted his face into a lopsided grin.

Jillian groaned, but snapped a shot anyway. She checked the photo and shook her head. "Funny."

And she wanted photos of the octopus.

"It just looks like a rock," David teased.

"But it's not a rock and that's the point," Jillian said. "She's hiding in plain sight, and I think that's cool."

They changed back to their street clothes and said thanks to Enid and Fairfax. It nagged at Jake that Priscilla didn't like him. What if the Earth's oceans were full of marine life that wouldn't like the Risonians?

Later, after the aquarium tour was finished and they were seated in the limo again, Jake told Jillian, "Don't publish the octopus photos. If people find out that Priscilla didn't like me and squirted me, they'll say that Earth's oceans reject the aliens from Rison."

Jillian disagreed. "You have to trust people. They'll just laugh about it if you put it out there now. You'll only be in trouble if you try to hide it."

Colonel Lett settled the question, "You can send the photos of the three of you. And even the one of the camouflaged octopus. But don't tell about the octopus squirting him."

Reluctantly, Jillian deleted the photo's caption and rewrote it to just state facts. "Today, we met a curled octopus named Priscilla."

I AM EMMELINE TULLIS

December 17

Em's eyes fluttered open to a blindingly white room. Bright overhead lights, white walls. She fingered the white sheets and fought to keep her fists from clutching at them in panic.

She was alone. Had been alone for days now.

Sick. Yes, sick. Vaguely, she remembered faces, but always the faces of strangers. Snatches of conversation, but in accents that confused her. Aliens. Had to be.

Alone.

Even in her dreams, her isolation turned on her. Restless dreams asked the same question: Who are you?

She answered:

I am Emmeline Tullis, adopted daughter of Randall and Beth Tullis.

I am Emmeline Tullis, sister to Marisa Tullis, dental assistant.

I am a swimmer, and a member of the Bainbridge Island swim team.

I am a freshman at Bainbridge Island High School.

I am the girlfriend of Jake Rose. Tears sprang to her eyes at that one and she amended it. I *was* the girlfriend of Jake Rose.

But any answer was hollow. Partly because she was alone, yes. But it was deeper. Perhaps every teenager comes to a place where they must reinvent themselves and decide who they are and what they believe in. But this felt more urgent. Something—the illness, the isolation, the aliens, the gut feeling that the very foundation of her world was shaken—something was desperately wrong.

Looking around her room—was this a hospital room?—she saw no windows, only white walls. White marble floors. One beige chair. No TV. No table for personal things. She had an IV in her right wrist. An extra blanket lay crookedly across the back of the beige chair.

Carefully, she pushed up to sitting, pausing to let a wave of dizziness pass. She was weak, too weak to get out of bed. Still sick, or just recuperating, she decided. She plumped up her pillow and carefully centered it exactly one inch below the head of the bed before lying back down. What kind of illness did she have? Why did the aliens get involved? Why was she all alone?

Quarantine. Her heart pounded in her ear.

She had been quarantined.

Panic threatened to swallow her, but she shoved it down and tried to think. Quarantined for what? Why aliens?

She shook her head—slowly to avoid another wave of dizziness. It didn't matter why. What mattered was to get out of here. Get this IV out. Get out of here. She was too weak, but she'd get stronger. And then, she'd get out of this white room. Because she had to find the answer to the question: Who are you?

The automatic answers came: I am Emmeline Tullis.

But the pat answer wasn't enough. Somehow, something had changed. Her subconscious knew something her conscious brain was too weak to understand.

Who was she?

THE JEWEL OF THE SEA

December 18
"Where now?" Colonel Lett asked.

Jillian tucked her blond hair into a knit cap and said hopefully, "Shopping?"

"Yes," Jake nodded. He wanted to hunt for Em, but they needed some idea of where to look for Phoke. Maybe just poking around the city for a while would help. He felt helpless because all he had was one word to go on—Phoke.

"Really?" Jillian said. "I didn't think you'd want to go shopping."

"For Mom's birthday," Jake said.

Of course, as a Risonian, Mom's actual date of birth wouldn't match up to Earth's calendar because of the differences in their planetary orbits. One Earth year is the amount of time it takes Earth to circle its star, Sol, which was 365 1/4 days; one Risonian year was the amount of time it takes Rison to circle its star, Turco, which was 414 days. When the diplomatic corps came from Rison, Earth insisted on birthdates on their documentation. Mom's self-proclaimed Earth-calendar birthday was later this month, December 28. Jake wanted to find the perfect gift.

"We should look at jewelry," Jillian said with enthusiasm. "When I travel, I always like to buy jewelry as souvenirs."

Jake thought about his Dad's *umjaadi* globes. His rooms, on the Moon or in the secret underwater Seastead installation, always included shelves for the water-filled globes from Rison. Similar to a snow-globe on Earth, Risonian vacation spots sold *umjaadi* globes as souvenirs. Mom had given Dad his first one, and after that, he'd collected many more. They were named for the *umjaadi* starfish that usually inhabited the globes. Jake wondered if there was something like that here, but doubted it. Jillian was probably right: jewelry was a good idea.

Colonel Lett drove carefully through the Edinburgh traffic—driving on the wrong side of the road, said Jillian, who was working on getting her driver's license back in Washington State—until he found a parking lot. They all climbed out and pulled on jackets against the December wind. Jake shook his head at Jillian, who wrapped a scarf around her neck and pulled the sock cap lower. As Risonians, they all had magma-sapiens metabolisms, which meant they seldom felt the cold weather. But the *paparazzi* were watching, and they didn't want to emphasize the differences in their species.

Jillian just shrugged and said defensively, "I think they look good on me."

Jake nodded and murmured, "Of course they do." He grabbed his string backpack that held his credit cards and id.

He stared upward at the massive Edinburgh castle. Grey stone, centuries old, sat majestically on the hillside and dominated the city. They would officially visit it later with Mom and see the Scottish crown jewels. For now, though, they headed down into the town in search of a jewelry store. Colonel Lett followed at a distance, letting the teens take the lead. It was comforting to know he was close by, Jake thought. Just in case.

Jillian stopped a couple times for selfies with the Edinburgh castle and Castle Rock in the background, and to take a couple group photos with David and Jake. The photos would be all over the Internet by nightfall, the way Jillian spread things around. The photos showed Jake, the Face of Rison, being just a normal teenager shopping for his mom's birthday present.

Jillian, who had accounts on all the social media platforms, was along partly to help spread the image that Jake was just a regular kid. She was a good counter-balance to the *paparazzi*, letting them control what photos were published. Jake didn't like it, but he understood it. It was all hollow stuff, but he allowed it dutifully.

Finally, Jillian pointed to a sign: Aberforth Jewelers.

As the group pushed in, a woman brushed past Jake. Something made him turn to watch her. She wore a heavy trench coat, and from the back of a red baseball cap swung a long length of blond hair.

"Ms. Fleming," called Jake. He was sure it was the biologist from Seattle who had helped him with a science class project about seals.

But the woman didn't turn around at his call.

Promptly, Colonel Lett was beside Jake. "Is there a problem?"

Jake shook his head. He must be crazy. Ms. Fleming was thousands of miles away in Seattle. No way would she'd be here in Edinburgh. "Nothing's wrong," he told Lett. "We'll just shop and be out in a while."

Stepping inside, someone called, "Hello! Welcome to Aberforth Jewelers."

A tall teenager, just a few years older than Jake, stood behind gleaming lighted cabinets that held a bewildering array of jewelry. If Jillian and David hadn't been with him, Jake would've backed out of the tiny, cramped store. The female's fondness for shopping was so puzzling to Jake. Maybe that was because on Rison he'd been the Prime Minister's step-son. No one expected Jake's family to go to the market or any store to shop. He just had to ask, and by afternoon, the things he wanted appeared in his room.

Perhaps another person would consider the shop to be cozy and comfortable. It was small, but warmly lit in spite of the dreary day. A small Christmas tree sparkled with crystal ornaments, and the lighted cabinets made the whole room glow. Maybe, Jake thought reluctantly, it would be okay to look around.

"Can I help you?" asked the teen.

"Did you know that lady that just left?" Jake asked. If it was Ms. Fleming—which of course, it wasn't—maybe she knew something about Em. It was just too much of a coincidence to find a familiar face in the city where Em might be held captive.

"Just a customer."

Jake grimaced. Even under the trench coat, the lady had seemed lean and had reminded him of the way Ms. Fleming walked. "Was she local or a tourist?"

The teenager shrugged. "Don't know. American, maybe. Anything else I can do for you?" He waved a hand toward the jewelry cases.

Jillian took charge. "Jake is looking for a birthday gift for his mom. He's not sure what he wants. Can you suggest something?"

The teen went into full sales mode, pulling out watches, bracelets and necklaces. Jillian and David hovered over the jewelry, but Jake wandered away. Somehow gold and silver didn't interest him. Even on Rison they had those metals, but they were only useful in technology, not as decorations for the body. Perhaps because volcanoes dominated their lives, Mom preferred glass created in a blazing hot furnace. Hence, the collectible *umjaadi* globes, made of the finest glass. Glass was cheap here on Earth, and often it looked cheap, too. Tizzalurian glass blowers were world-renowned — Jake stopped his thoughts short. Maybe world-renowned on Rison, but not interstellar-renowned. Their reputation would die with the planet when Rison imploded. He wondered if any of the glass blowers had been evacuated to the Cadee Moon Base on Rison's moon, or if any were slated to come to Earth. That is, if Earth ever decided to let Risonians live on their planet.

Jake stopped at a case full of a golden rock or stone. When there was a break in the other's conversation, Jake asked, "What's this stone?"

"Ah, amber," said the teen. Apparently, it was a subject that fascinated him because he got chatty. He drifted over to stand behind the cabinet that held only the amber jewelry. "By the way, my name's Matt Meacher. Let me tell you all about amber. They call it the jewel of the sea."

Amber was the fossilized resin from ancient forests that now lay under the North Sea. It wasn't produced from tree sap, Matt explained, but rather from plant resin. The aromatic resin dripped from and oozed down trees, often filling internal cracks, trapping debris such as seeds, leaves, feathers and insects. Especially insects. Amber was made popular by an American author's stories about dinosaurs made from blood found in mosquitoes that were trapped in amber. Michael Crichton's "Jurassic Park" stories had been a boon for amber jewelry sales, according to Matt. Jake had read those stories, as fascinated by the dinosaurs as any Earthling.

"Do you think your mom would like a pin or a necklace or a bracelet?" Jillian asked.

"Necklace," Jake said.

Jillian pointed to something and Matt pulled it out, arranging it on a piece of dark blue velvet. When he pulled his hand back, Jake gasped. A delicately carved, golden amber mermaid seemed to be swimming across a deep blue sea. Her tail swirled in a flamboyant curve, and her exotic hair fell to her waist.

"May I?" Jake nodded to the mermaid.

At Matt's nod in agreement, Jake picked up the carved amber and turned it over and over. It was only an inch and a half long. Polished smooth, it gleamed in his hands. He remembered the last birthday party he'd attended for Mom. The Quad-des knew how to throw a party, and they had invited about 1000 people. He'd spent a long time creating a special set of music files for Mom, ordered in a specific way, and writing a commentary on the whole thing. She made the band play his list for the rest of the night. And for the next year, Mom listened to the music over and over. It had been a great feeling to get it right. Since he'd left Rison for the Obama Moon Base, he hadn't been at one of her birthday parties. This year, there probably wouldn't even be a party with all the negotiations going on. But he wanted to get the present right again. And this necklace was perfect.

Jillian had her hands on her hips and wore a grin of self-satisfaction. "Beautiful." She whipped out her phone and said, "Hold it up. And try not to grimace so much."

Reluctantly, Jake let her snap a photo. Another frowning image of the Face of Rison to spread far and wide. Mom never looked at Jillian's accounts, so there was little chance that she'd see the amber necklace before he gave it to her next week.

"Would you like that gift wrapped?"

Jillian nodded. "He's all thumbs when he tries to wrap."

Jake said firmly, "I'll take two of them gift wrapped." At Jillian's puzzled look, he said, "One for Mom and one for Em."

"Ah. So, your mom and girlfriend will match."

"Are you being sarcastic?" Jake said, totally puzzled.

Jillian raised her eyebrows. "Yes."

Crestfallen, Jake said, "Won't they both like it?" He hadn't had a chance to give Em a birthday gift yet, but he wanted to be ready. In fact, he didn't even know when her birthday was. As soon as he found her, he'd have to ask.

"Sure," Jillian said, and shook her head while posting the photos to her accounts.

Jake sighed to himself again. He'd never figure out girls.

Matt took the mermaid necklaces through a curtained doorway to be wrapped. When he came back out, he went to the cash register to take Jake's credit card. This was one of the nice changes about being known as the Risonian Ambassador's son. When he was hiding on Bainbridge Island, Jake could have no digital footprint: no cell phones, no credit cards, nothing. But now, he had credit cards that were accepted worldwide.

David wandered the aisles of jewelry until he stopped in front of a stack of colorful postcards and picked one up. Glancing at it, his eyes went wide. "Jake, you gotta see this."

Jake took the postcard, but had to sign the sales receipt first. When he turned over the postcard, his heart ran cold.

Phoke. It was word that Em had scrawled on Dr. Bari's business card.

Phoke. In parentheses was the pronunciation (FO-key).

It was for a folk band, he realized. And they were playing at the Marco Polo Pub that night from 8 to midnight.

Stunned, Jake turned to Matt. "Have you heard this band?"

David and Jillian stood at Jake's elbows. To keep him calm, Jake thought. That was a wise thing for them to do because his hope of finding Em had suddenly soared. He'd listen to a million bands if it would lead him to Em.

"They are pretty good," Matt said. "Folk music, you know, based a lot on old Scottish and Celtic music."

"What does it mean, Phoke?" Jillian asked.

"Ah, Phoke," Matt said. "There are many legends around here of the Mer folk. You know, mermaids and mermen." He waved a hand in the air, as if to dismiss the legends as trivial. "But teenagers have to come up with their own jargon. Everyone on Earth knows of Nike, the Greek word that means 'win.' If you wear Nike shoes or clothes, you're likely to win. So, someone started calling the Mer folk, the Phoke, which is Greek for 'seals.' You know, the sea animals."

"Phoke means the mermaids?" David asked doubtfully.

Matt shrugged. "I kinda like it. Updates that ancient term, 'mermaid.' Don't ya think?"

"Are there really Phoke around here?" David asked.

"Depends on who you talk with," Matt put his elbows on the glass counter top and rested his chin in his hands, staring at the trio. Hesitantly, he said, "Are you interested in getting to Aberforth?"

From the back, an older man came through the curtained doorway carrying two gift-wrapped packages with golden bows.

Confused, David said, "I thought we were in the Aberforth Jewelers."

"Matt! Have you cleaned fingerprints off the glass counters yet today?"

Jake turned around, surprised by the sharp tone of the older man.

"Ah. I'll do that now." Looking embarrassed, Matt pushed back and went to put away the jewelry that he'd brought out to show Jake.

The older man held out the boxes, which made Jake switch the postcard from his right to his left hand. Jake put them into his string backpack, along with the postcard.

"What's that, then?" the man asked.

"Postcard for the Phoke band." Jake held out the card. "Thought we might go to listen tonight. We'll see if mermen and mermaids can make music."

The man turned slightly to glare at Matt.

"Not very good music. Save yourself the bother," the man said.

Suddenly suspicious, Jake asked, "Where is this Aberforth everyone talks about?"

Without a word, the older man turned and stomped away.

"Did we get you in trouble somehow?" Jillian whispered to Matt.

"Nah. He'll calm down." Matt squirted glass cleaner on a jewelry cabinet and then used a towel to rub the cabinet top. "Best be going your way, though."

"Thanks for the info. We'll go to that pub tonight," Jake told him. "I want to know more about the Phoke."

Matt nodded solemnly, "Enjoy the music."

FISH AND CHIPS

December 18

Across the pub, Jake waved at Enid Ways. His mom was busy with political negotiations tonight, so she couldn't come along to hear the Phoke band. Colonel Lett could get them in the pub—and make sure they only drank soft drinks—but Mom had wanted some local person to supervise, also. Enid had been happy at the suggestion of listening to the band.

The pub was dark, crowded and a sensory overload—perfect for Jillian and David, but overwhelming to Jake who had been isolated on the moon for a couple years, and still craved that kind of privacy.

Enid had arrived early and saved them a padded booth close to the music. At her suggestion, they ordered fish and chips.

Jake sat back to watch the band. With a guitar, violin, and vocalist, it had a surprisingly Irish sound. Or was that Scottish? Jake wasn't sure of the differences; he only knew it wasn't American. The percussion was a handheld, animal-skinned drum, a traditional *bodhrán*, Enid explained. A dark-haired guy with dreads used a single stick to thump it in a vibrant rhythm. There was a flavor of folk music style, combined with a livelier rock sound—a fusion of old and new. Which was probably the point of the band, to update the old tunes.

When the order came, Jake stared at the greasy paper holding the fish and chips. They were just French fries and fish sticks, Jake thought. Hesitantly, he took a bite. Fortunately, they tasted much better than any French fries he'd had in Seattle.

The music was too loud for real conversation, and Jake, Jillian and David were hungry after a busy day. They concentrated on eating and listening.

When the band finally took an intermission, though, Enid leaned over and asked, "What did you think of Priscilla today?"

"The real question," Jake said, "is why she didn't like me."

Enid's brow wrinkled. "You're right. I've never seen her spray anyone before."

"Do you think it's because I'm Risonian? Or could it be something else?"

"Who knows? We don't have the research to answer that. Maybe you ate garlic yesterday and that made your skin taste bad." Enid's curls bounced as she shook her head. "No way to know."

"The octopus makes me wonder about life on Earth. Why do humans live on land and not in the sea? We're so similar and yet so different."

Enid laughed, "You're talking about mermaids and mermen."

"I've read the stories," Jake said sheepishly. He had hoped to get information by hinting at more, but Enid saw through that. "Are they real?"

"As an oceanographer, I wonder that, too," Enid said. "Since the Risonians are asking to come to Earth, I've even looked at the old research to see if there's anything but myths." She shook her head. "If there are mermen, they know how to hide."

"Like Priscilla camouflaging herself and hiding in plain sight?"

She shrugged and spread out her hands. "You could go swimming in the North Sea and look around for yourself." She laughed, a musical sound, and her eyes twinkled in the muted light. "If you find anything, let me know."

By now, the band was back and the music started again. Jillian pulled Jake to the dance floor. He found himself posing for more selfies, wondering what he was doing in Edinburgh, and if he'd ever see Em again. He hoped that Jillian wasn't taking a video of him wiggling his body around in strange ways.

Then across the crowd, he caught a glimpse of a lady who looked like Bobbie Fleming. It must be the same lady they saw coming out of the jewelry store. Surely, it wasn't the biologist from Seattle, but Jake wanted a closer look. She was drinking something frothy and talking intently with a dark-haired man. Now, both nodded, as if they had agreed on something.

Jake dragged Jillian through the crowd.

The lady locked eyes with him. She wore wire-rimmed glasses exactly like Bobbie Fleming. It must be her, or her doppelgänger.

The woman spun away and shoved through the crowd as if avoiding them.

The band started a new song, apparently a favorite tune because the crowd stepped closer to the stage, closing up any gaps for Jake and Jillian to squeeze through. Jake still pushed along, but it was like moving against an avalanche. He made progress, but so slowly that he felt like he was standing still.

Finally, the song ended and they had made it to the opposite side of the room. But the Bobbie Fleming lookalike was gone. A chill ran though him, as if an important clue had slipped through his fingers.

Disappointed, Jake spun and scanned the room. He felt himself drooping, not from tiredness but from frustration. The Phoke band was interesting, but he didn't see how any of this related to Em and her disappearance. It was a dead end.

HAGGIS AND BAGPIPES

December 19

Jake woke to a screeching sound that he recognized. He threw a pillow over his head and said, "Colonel Lett, turn it off."

The bagpipe music continued.

With a sigh, Jake rolled over and sat up, rubbing his eyes.

"Good," Colonel Lett said gruffly and tapped his phone to stop the music. "The Ambassador asks you to attend a luncheon with her."

Jake groaned. But he had to play his role as the teenage Face of Rison. At least, he'd been free half a day yesterday and last evening, even if it led him no closer to finding Em. Mom was making sure he had time to enjoy Edinburgh, so he couldn't complain about this luncheon.

When Mom came in later, Jake was dressed and ready. Colonel Lett reported that Jillian was still asleep. Surprisingly, though, David arrived and said that he hoped to go along, too.

"Is this an important luncheon?" Jake asked Mom.

Ambassador Quad-de wore a red business suit, which accented her curly dark hair and dark eyes. "Yes. The Lord Provost Kin Coombe is hosting the world leaders who are here at my request." At Jake's raised eyebrow, she added, "Lord Provost is like a city mayor. They just have ceremonial titles." She gave a laugh. "His full title is Lord Provost Kin Coombe, the Lord-Lieutenant of Edinburgh and the Admiral of the Firth of Forth."

David rolled his eyes. "Can we say pretentious?"

"No," Mom said more seriously. "It's just their custom. Americans wouldn't add on titles like that, of course. But it's tradition for the Brits."

Jake wanted to laugh at David because he was so American. It was good, he thought, that David didn't know Jake's full Risonian name and titles. Tizzalurians, it seemed, were just as bad as Brits.

Their hotel was on a hill, and as they walked out, they stopped to look over the city. Like Rome and other famous cities, Edinburgh was built across seven hills. Edinburgh castle filled the hilltop to the south, and the tallest hill to the north was empty. Between was a big valley. The meeting this morning was in a government building, quite old, made of quarried marble and limestone. The vestibule echoed, and they climbed a shallow set of steps toward a little-used formal ballroom. Long tables were set in a U-shape and decorated with vases of elaborate Christmas arrangements. At the head table, places were set for the Lord Provost, the Risonian ambassador, and the highest-ranking officials attending. Jake and David were seated at the end of a long table, almost as far away from Jake's mom as possible.

After locating their seating arrangement, Jake wanted to just sit and watch people. Instead, David insisted they mingle. Without fear, he marched up to people, introduced himself and Jake, and started chatting. They met the aides for the French ambassador, the Belgian under-ambassador, and the Portuguese ambassador's wife. Jake was amazed that they all spoke perfect English. It was truly the business language of this world. But when David broke into some Portuguese, the ambassador's wife, Leonara Zalarich, was truly pleased. They chatted for several minutes, leaving Jake in the dark. Jake, like most Risonians, spoke several languages, but he'd chosen Russian, Mandarin Chinese, Hindi, and English — not European languages. Even educated here on Earth, Commander Gordon had demanded that David be multi-lingual; besides English, David spoke Spanish, Portuguese, French, and German — all European languages.

It wasn't just his choice of languages that impressed Jake, though. David was at ease in starting a conversation and in keeping the interest of these international leaders. He knew all their names and had appropriate questions about their stance on Rison or other politics of their lands.

In a flash of jealousy, Jake thought, *David should've been the ambassador's son, not me*. He remembered that Commander Gordon's sister, David's aunt, had been killed when Europe shot down the *Fullex*, a Risonian vessel with about 500 evacuees. They claimed that the *Fullex* had violated Earth's space without permission, and it was considered an act of war. David couldn't mention that incident, of course, without coming out of character as a human teen just tagging along with a Risonian teen. But maybe he had inherited his aunt's abilities as a politician.

During the opening reception, bagpipe music played. Jake actually liked it. He'd first heard it from the school bus driver back on Bainbridge, and they'd struck up a friendship sharing musical tracks they both liked. Here the bagpipes were playing on a balcony at the far end of the huge room, so they weren't overwhelming—fortunately.

At each table setting was a printed sheet with the names and titles of those attending. Jake glanced through it and realized that he'd heard Mom talk about most of them at one time or another. So when they sat, Jake was surprised that the old woman who sat on his right was someone he'd never heard of before.

"I'm Lady Zuzanna Coombe. The Lord Provost is my son," she said simply. Amazingly, she acted upon her self-appointed tour guide status by explaining everything.

The meal began with a priest giving a blessing. "Some hae meat and canna eat, and some would eat that want it. But we hae meat, and we can eat, Sae let the Lord be thankit."

Zuzanna said, "That's a traditional prayer, you know. It comes from our poet, Robert Burns. Next will come the haggis. It's quite a show."

At David's arched eyebrow, she added, "It's traditional Scottish food: a pudding made of the heart, liver, and such, of a sheep or calf, minced with suet and oatmeal, seasoned, and boiled in the stomach of the animal."

Jake made a face. "And do you like haggis?"

She leaned closer and said, "Hate it." She shrugged. "Doesn't matter. It's tradition and you have to take the good with the bad when you live by tradition."

Jake laughed, "That's true." He knew exactly what she meant because tradition ruled his stepfather's life, too. Swann always railed against the comment, "We've never done it that way before."

"100 years from now," Swann always said, "They'll moan about a tradition that I started. And I hope they break that tradition if it no longer makes sense in their world."

For the haggis, everyone stood, while the bagpipe players marched down from the balcony and played with gusto.

The Lord Provost held a carved dagger high and recited Lord Robert Burns's poem, "Address to a Haggis."

Fair fa' your honest, sonsie face,
Great chieftain o' the pudding-race!
Aboon them a' yet tak your place,
Painch, tripe, or thairm:
Weel are ye wordy o'a grace
As lang's my arm.

The groaning trencher there ye fill,
Your hurdies like a distant hill,
Your pin was help to mend a mill
In time o'need,
While thro' your pores the dews distil
Like amber bead.

His knife see rustic Labour dight,
An' cut you up wi' ready sleight,

Brandishing the dagger, the Lord Provost dramatically thrust downward and pierced the haggis, releasing a spicy smell that surprised Jake. It might actually taste OK.

Trenching your gushing entrails bright,
Like ony ditch;
And then, O what a glorious sight,
Warm-reekin', rich!

Jake understood only half of the old Scottish, but loved the lilt and the vigor of the delivery. The poem continued a few more stanzas, but Jake was more interested in watching the spectators. The group was widely varied, representatives from around the world. Everyone watched the Scottish spectacle with interest. As the poem came to a climax, the servant held high the platter of haggis.

The Lord Provost grabbed his wine glass and yelled, "The Haggis!"

Everyone echoed his yell, "The Haggis!"

Then laughter erupted around the room. It was a welcome relief of the tension, a welcome contrast to the solemn occasion and the intensity of the emotions in the room.

They ate. Jake sampled the sliced haggis, and Lady Coombe laughed when he quietly spit it out. It might smell good, but it didn't taste good. Some of the other Scottish dishes were delicious, though. He especially loved the shortbread cookies at the end.

After the meal, the Lord Provost insisted that everyone stand and hold hands in a circle. He began *a cappella*, singing Robert Burn's song, "Auld Lang Syne." A quartet joined him, though, and carried the remainder of the song:

Should auld acquaintance be forgot,
And never brought to mind?
Should auld acquaintance be forgot,
And auld lang syne!

For auld lang syne, my dear,
For auld lang syne.
We'll tak a cup o' kindness yet,
For auld lang syne.

Jake realized that he needed to go back into the city and find the Robert Burns memorial tower to learn more about this Scotsman.

The circle broke apart with applause and laughter.

Next the crowd moved into a grand parlor, as Lady Coombe called it. Here, Mom would give her plea for help. Lady Coombe sat beside Jake and David again, still playing tour guide, while Colonel Lett stood rigidly nearby alert for any signs of danger.

Mom stood to give her speech, her red suit a splash of color in the sedate room. Her voice carried well, and she was organized. "We ask you to lift the blockade and allow Risonian ships to land on Earth. We readily admit the crisis is of our own making from when we tampered with nature by trying to stop volcanoes from exploding. It was foolish to use Brown Matter. But the reality is that our planet's core is disappearing into a black hole. She'll implode. Earth and Risonian scientists agree that there's no way to stop it. But you can stop the overwhelming loss of an entire species, race and culture." She followed with a well-worn series of arguments; she was just more emotional this time. She talked about a couple of the people lost on the *Fullex*, the Risonian immigrant ship that had been shot down, and ended with a plea: "I urge you to vote with compassion. Please. You only live on land, and Earth is 70% water. Allow Risonians to live in the seas."

Polite smiles dampened the ambassador's passion, but here and there, a wife or an under-ambassador wiped away a tear.

David whispered to Jake, "She's good. Very good."

Jake nodded. Of course she was good at what she did. Their family had always been in politics, and from childhood, Dayexi had been trained for just this sort of thing. Sadly, Jake reflected, his own training had been interrupted by the threat of Rison's implosion when they had sent him to live with his biological father stationed on a Navy base on Earth's moon. He didn't think he had the right sort of personality for politics, anyway.

Trying to be a better ambassador's son, Jake pulled out an ink pen and jotted notes beside names on the roster, trying to remember snatches of conversation. Odd things that would make him remember either the person or some small detail about them. For example the Portuguese ambassador's wife, Leonara Zalarich, wore only rubies or red jewels. A small thing, but maybe someday that small bit of knowledge would give them an opening they needed. You had to connect with people and one way to do that was to remember what was important to them. She wouldn't be a fan, for example, of the amber jewelry he had bought for his mother and Em yesterday.

But Jake quickly exhausted his meager knowledge of the politicians. Frustrated, he doodled while mentally reviewing the problems of the Risonians: they had to find refuge or face extinction. But even if Earth allowed them to live in the seas, would they get along with humans?

A rousing applause brought him back to the moment. He clapped woodenly, anxiously studying faces. Had Mom convinced anyone? Changed anyone's mind?

Lady Coombe nudged his elbow. "You dropped this, I believe."

Jake looked down at the roster to see that he'd drawn Em's face over and over.

"Who is she?" asked the old woman.

Frowning, Jake deliberately folded the paper, hiding Em's face and put it in his jacket pocket. "Just a friend." His voice was cold, discouraging more questions.

Lady Coombe took the hint. She stood, took his hand, and dropped a quick curtsy. "It's been a pleasure getting to visit with you, young Risonian. Is there anything else I can explain or help you with?"

Jake bowed formally in return. He hesitated, but he needed information. "Where is Aberforth?"

"Aberforth Hills, you mean," she answered promptly. "My Granny used to tell stories about that. It's a Mer folk story, about their underwater city. Edinburgh is built on seven hills and Aberforth Hills is supposed to be built on seven underwater hills."

At Jake's look of surprise, she chanted:

"Abbey, Calton, Castle Grand,
Southward see St. Leonards stand,
St, Johns and Sciennes as two are given,
And Multrees makes Seven."

She looked toward the ceiling, as if some answer was written above. "There used to be another rhyme for the seven hills of Aberforth Hills, but I can't remember it now." She tapped a finger on her lips as if that might make the rhyme appear.

Startled that she actually had information, Jake pressed for more. "Are the Mer folk the same as the Phoke?"

"I've heard that name lately. I think the teenagers call the mermaids and mermen, the Phoke." She shrugged. "I guess it's the same."

"The Mer folk—they're not real?" Jake said tentatively.

"Myth," agreed the old lady. "But it's a persistent myth here along the North Sea."

Jake remembered the conversation with Enid about mermen. He asked, "Any idea where Aberforth Hills is located? If it's real, that is."

"The North Sea," said Lady Coombe. Her eyes twinkled and her lips twitched as if they wanted to smile.

Jake laughed. "That doesn't help."

Lady Coombe pursed her lips and cocked her head, as if in thought. Finally, she said, "My Granny grew up in St. Abbs. Go fishing at St. Abbs. Try the Merlin Charters."

Jake and David looked at each other and nodded. Tomorrow, they'd go to St. Abbs.

FAMILY

December 19

The door to Em's hospital room shoved open, swinging silently inward.

Em pulled herself upright and winced at how the effort strained her reserve energy. She recognized the blond woman with wire-rimmed glasses as the marine biologist from Bainbridge Island. Confused, she struggled to remember her name. "Miss Fleming?"

The woman pushed up her glasses and asked, "Emily. Um, Em, are you okay? I've been worried."

"Fine," Em shrugged. "Except no one will answer any questions."

"Like what?"

"Where are my parents? Why can't I see them?" Em's voice was ragged with frustration and anger. Why had the aliens allowed this woman here? Why not her parents? And besides that, what she really wanted to ask was, "Where is Jake?" She had mixed feelings about him, but mostly she just wanted for him to walk in the door and make her laugh.

"Yes," Ms. Fleming said. "You need answers. It's time you had answers."

"I know you won't know anything, but the doctors and nurses—" Em trailed off at Ms. Fleming's nod of understanding. Her hair, tied up in a ponytail, nodded, also. Em noticed now that Fleming wore a hospital gown, terry-cloth robe and house slippers. She must be a patient here, too, for some reason. What were the aliens doing to her?

"But I do know something," Ms. Fleming said.

Em nodded cautiously. If Ms. Fleming had answers, maybe she was an alien, too. Being a marine biologist—it made sense if she was Risonian.

Ms. Fleming looked around. "We need somewhere to talk, but there's no place to sit here. Do you feel like a ride in a wheelchair?"

"Yes!" Em had been out walking in the hallway with Shelby Bulmer, a nurse's aide, at her side. He had held her arm to keep her wobbly knees from giving way. But she'd only had the strength to walk to the nurse's station and back, a couple hundred feet at best. A wheelchair would get her out of this horrible room. Everything in this crazy hospital was white: white floors, white walls, white hallways, white uniforms, white sheets, and white hospital gowns. Whoever built it was one strange alien. Em desperately craved color.

Ms. Fleming returned a moment later with a wheelchair and helped Em get settled in it before she pushed out into the hallway. They went the opposite direction from the nurse's station out into another hallway. Apparently, Ms. Fleming knew her way around this place, this alien installation.

She stopped at a doorway that read: Observation Room.

"Are you ready?" Ms. Fleming asked.

"For what?"

"For this." Ms. Fleming pushed into a room that was dimly lit. The far wall was a floor-to-ceiling window and beyond the window were city lights. But—a fish swam by the window.

"We're underwater?" Em's voice rose an octave in excitement. Her dim memory of being in a pod that dove deep underwater, it hadn't been a dream. How long had the Risonians been on Earth? To build something like this, they must have come right after first contact.

"Yes. About 250 feet under water," Ms. Fleming replied.

Ms. Fleming parked the wheelchair beside the window, where Em could overlook the city. She reached for the wheels and adjusted the chair to be exactly perpendicular to the window.

Em looked from the city to Ms. Fleming, and said flatly, "You're one of them."

Ms. Fleming's eyes widened in surprise. She nodded agreement.

Em jabbed her finger at Ms. Fleming and accused, "You're aliens from Rison, right? How long have you been in our oceans already?"

"What? Aliens?" Ms. Fleming shook her head, and her eyebrows were drawn in confusion.

Em nodded. "I figured it out. Dr. Bari brought me down here in some sort of pod or something. He wasn't wearing scuba gear, and the only creatures that can breathe in the ocean are the aliens from Rison."

Ms. Fleming pulled up a chair, positioned its back to the window—exactly parallel—and sat straddling the chair with her arms resting on the chair's back. "I can see why you'd think that. But this culture is much older. It's ancient."

"You mean aliens have been on Earth for years?" Em's voice squeaked in surprise.

"No. We're the Mer folk."

Em drew a blank and shook her head slightly. "What?"

"Mermaids and mermen," said Ms. Fleming.

Em stared from Ms. Fleming to the city lights outside the window. A school of halibut dashed past the window. "You've got to be kidding," Em said. Believing in aliens was hard enough. Believing in mermaids and mermen—well, it was ridiculous. She waved at the buildings and tunnels and—"What am I looking at here?"

Ms. Fleming said, "Light pollution."

Instantly, Em understood what Ms. Fleming meant. At a depth of 250 feet, there should be no light. But the scene in front of her was like a major city lit up at night. The buildings nearest their building—a hospital, she assumed—varied in height from what looked like one story to maybe five or six stories. Part of that height difference seemed to be the age of the building, with the smaller buildings looking older. The smallest was obviously made of some metal, but the surface had aged a dirty green and it looked pitted with age. Salt water would be a brutal environment for building materials. It was also a strange shape, like an upside down brass bell.

She responded, "The city looks old."

Ms. Fleming said, "Yes. Aberforth Hills is 100 years old, or thereabouts."

Now, Em was starting to see beyond the nearby buildings and trying to make sense of what lay beyond. The hospital was clearly built on a hill that gave them a wide view of the underwater city. Instead of streets, the buildings were connected with tunnels, and Em could dimly see figures moving in the tunnels. This was fascinating. But Mer?

"Um, are you sure this is a Mer folk city and not an alien city? Do you know any of the Mer?"

Ms. Fleming's blue eyes were solemn. Frizzy wisps of hair escaped her tight ponytail and framed her face. She said, "I am one."

Em whirled around to stare. "Wait. You're a mermaid?" she said skeptically.

Ms. Fleming said simply, "Yes."

"Oh." Em appreciated that Ms. Fleming was doing this in an understated way and allowing her time to process the startling information. But did she really think that Em would believe it?

"You mean you could walk out the door—no, swim out—however you get out—and just swim around all you want out there? Where's your tail?"

"No tails, that's all a myth. Our anatomy is different than humans, and we have limitations. But yes, basically, I could go swimming around out there in the city whenever I wanted."

"Oh." Em wondered if she had fallen down Alice-in-Wonderland's hole or something. "You're serious."

"It's a fact."

"Wait." Em put some information together and said, "Your brother is Dr. Bari, right. Is he a merman?"

Ms. Fleming nodded.

Bong! Trying to locate the sound, Em realized that it came from a tall tower that lay straight ahead. Bong! It seemed to hold a huge clock, sort of like Big Ben in London. Bong!

"Is that ringing the hour?" she asked incredulously.

"That's the Gunby School Clock Tower. We call it The Gunby. And yes, it's ringing the hour. School is just letting out."

"School?" Em closed her eyes and tried to process the whole thing. This was a secret mermaid and merman city and they had a school and a hospital, and a marine biologist like Ms. Fleming, someone who called herself a scientist, was admitting to being a mermaid.

"Am I hallucinating?" she murmured. She closed her eyes and ran a hand over her forehead.

"I'm sorry. This isn't the way I wanted to tell you," Ms. Fleming said, her voice deep with regret. "I imagined this so many times, but never like this." She waved a hand at the wheelchair.

Still massaging her temples, Em said wearily. "Why am I here? Will I wake up in the morning and this will all be a dream?"

"Your illness is water borne and the Mer doctors know more about it than anyone else." Ms. Fleming said.

At that, Em looked up in relief. "Oh. That makes sense. If there were such as thing as Mer folk, they would specialize in water-borne illnesses. I'm getting better, right?"

"Yes," Ms. Fleming said. But her forehead was creased, and she didn't meet Em's eyes.

Suddenly homesick, Em said, "Where are my parents?"

"Ah, that's a problem." Ms. Fleming waved at the city in front of them, "Aberforth Hills is in the North Sea, off the coast of Scotland, the northern part of England."

Em felt almost numb with shock. "North Sea?"

"Yes. I arrived yesterday in Edinburgh, Scotland. I came out to Aberforth Hills this morning."

Scotland? Em was in a Mer folk hospital because she had a water-borne illness and that hospital was half a world away from Seattle. "Mom," she whispered. "I want my mom."

Ms. Fleming stood and patted Em's shoulder. "It's a lot to take in, I know. I know. They won't let your adopted mother come here. But she knows you're safe and that you're getting expert treatment. We'll ask Dr. Bari later and see if you can telephone her."

Em looked up in despair. Ms. Fleming's face was pale. Desperately Em wished for someone else to talk with, someone calmer. But Ms. Fleming was her only option. Em took a shuddering breath and said stoically, "So. I am kidnapped. By the Mer folk."

"No! We're just trying to help you get well."

"Then I can leave whenever I want? Or my Mom and Dad can come and get me?"

Ms. Fleming sat again in the chair and stared out at the city. The tunnels were busier with figures walking back and forth now. Em supposed that with school out, families were going to pick up children's and then maybe do some shopping. Did they have shops underwater here? They must. A city this size, they couldn't run up to the surface for bread and milk. Was she really starting to accept that this underwater city belonged to Mer people?

"Can Mom pick me up later today?"

"About that." Ms. Fleming turned decisively in her chair and leaned toward Em.

A stab of fear shot through Em. "Are they OK? Did they get this illness, too?"

"No, no, nothing like that."

"Then, what?"

"This is hard." Ms. Fleming cleared her throat, held out a hand toward Em, and then let it fall back into her lap. "You know you're adopted?"

"Of course." Mom and Dad had never hidden that from her or her adopted sister, Marisa. They grew up knowing that they'd been specially chosen for the Tullis family.

"Do you know anything about your real parents?" Ms. Fleming asked.

"My biological parents," Em corrected. "No. I have a necklace they gave me but nothing else."

"Let me tell you a story about a boy and a girl—"

Em broke in. "My parent's love story and how they didn't love me?" She'd read enough about reunion stories to know how this went. It was the Romeo and Juliet thing, where they shouldn't have ever met. But it was a great love. Except, they didn't love enough to stick it out and create a family for their baby. She didn't need this story.

Ms. Fleming winced. "It's not quite like that."

"From their point of view, maybe. But it's fair from my point of view." Em's face was rigid and her stomach cramped. She'd often dreamed of the chance to say that to her biological mother. Giving up a child, it was a cruel.

Ms. Fleming whispered. "Still, will you hear me out?"

Em shrugged. A sudden weariness settled over her, probably from the illness and the shock of her situation. She needed to sleep. "Whatev."

But Ms. Fleming turned back to the city without talking.

Em closed her eyes and sighed. She needed to go back to her room.

At last, Ms. Fleming asked in a low voice: "Have you ever met a Mer before?"

Em yawned, so weary that she didn't even raise her hand to hide her open mouth. "Not that I know of."

"Good answer," Ms. Fleming said. "Because I'm sure you have and you just didn't know it. The problem with living hidden like the Mer folk do is that you get isolated. But we don't like that. We like to meet people and have fun and—well, you know that story about mermaids singing and enchanting men?"

"Everyone knows that myth," Em said dismissing it with a casual wave of her hand.

"But did you know that human men are also sirens for mermaids? For some mermaids, the experience of meeting a human male is overwhelming. It's like what you read about in a love story, where someone sweeps you off your feet." She paused. "That happened to me. I was swept off my feet by Damien Fleming. He charmed me from the first moment we met. Not that he knew it. It was high school, and he didn't really see me till we met again in college." Softly, almost to herself, she added, "I always loved his laugh."

"And?" Em fidgeted impatiently with the tie on her white terry cloth robe.

"And he wanted me to marry him. I couldn't."

"Why not?" Em asked because it was expected of her, not that she really cared.

"My brother wouldn't let me." Ms. Fleming's voice was hard and flat.

Em threw up her hands, incredulous. "You let your brother stop you from marrying the man you loved?"

Ms. Fleming shrugged. "I'm half-Mer. Many of the Mer folk are only one-fourth Mer or less. Our race is slowly being threatened by marrying outsiders. Those of us with at least half-Mer blood, we swore to marry only Mer, to have only Mer babies. It wouldn't have been bad. It's rather like countries where there's an arranged marriage, you know."

Em thought about that. While she still wasn't convinced this was all true, it was more interesting than she'd expected. "So, when a human male comes along and falls in love with one of you, you're not allowed to marry. Wow!"

"That's it," Ms. Fleming said. "Except, I loved Damien. And we were going to get married anyway. Before I could talk my brother into it, though, I got pregnant."

They stared at each other, and Em wondered if Ms. Fleming's blue eyes were going to spill over with tears. And then, her own eyes filled. Em felt suddenly like she was poised at the top of a diving platform—the highest platform ever built. And someone was about to shove her off and the fall would forever change her life.

Slowly, as if each word weighed a thousand pounds, Fleming said, "You're my daughter. You're a mermaid, and it's time you claimed your heritage."

NEGOTIATIONS

December 20

The speedboat powered over the choppy waves of the harbor and headed out into the chilly North Sea. Jake and his mother stood beside the rail and stared at the grey waters. Colonel Lett was driving the boat while Colonel Barbena leaned on the opposite rail. The smell of seawater and fish was strong, comforting. Jake needed that just now because they were headed into danger.

"Are you sure this is wise?" Jake asked again, worry cramping his stomach. He had hoped to go to St. Abbs with David and Jillian today, but Mom had insisted that Jake accompany her on another official visit.

Mom shrugged. She always loved the wind at sea. But in this sharp wind, she wrinkled her nose, which made her Risonian nose ridges more prominent. "General Puentes asked for this meeting. We have to try to make peace with him."

"But he was Cyrus Hill's commander. He's in charge of the ELLIS Forces that tried to capture you all last year."

ELLIS stood for Earth-LLGlobular Star Cluster Interstellar Security force, and it was created soon after Earth's first contact with the planet Rison, which is located in that star cluster.

"It's worse than that," Mom said quietly.

"Yes, when I was up against Cyrus Hill, I researched them online. I found Hill's and Puentes's connection," Jake said. "Coach Blevins and General Puentes are brothers-in-law, married to sisters. Both wives are dead now, but they've kept the connection strong."

Mom nodded. "General Puentes is Cyrus Hill's uncle. Hill is taking care of Coach Blevins, who has a degenerative human disease called Parkinsons. Hill and Blevins are out of the picture for a while."

That surprised Jake. A month ago, he'd overheard Coach and Cy talking about a doctor's visit. But he hadn't known it would progress so quickly. He was sorry Coach was sick, but he was glad he wouldn't meet either Coach or Cy again. "So—

why meet with Puentes? He's definitely an enemy, and not a politician. It could be a trap."

Mom leaned on the rail and shrugged. Glancing sideways, she said, "It's the Tizzalurian way. If we were from the Bo-See Coalition in the South, well, we'd have invaded Earth already. It's a good thing they didn't have the technology to build interstellar space ships."

"The aliens come in peace," murmured Jake ironically. But would General Puentes accept them in peace?

Mom straightened up and stretched. She turned around and her face lit up. "Look!"

It was late afternoon, and in the distance a bank of clouds threatened an evening shower. The sun was at the perfect angle, and a rainbow splayed across the sky. Jake had only seen partial rainbows, but this one was a perfect arc, a complete rainbow. It was still one of the wonders of Earth for him.

"Peace," Mom said firmly. "Whatever else, we need to find peace with all humans. We have to go to this meeting. I'm hopeful that General Puentes is also seeking peace."

Jake wanted to add, "And if he's not?" But he stopped himself. They had their bodyguards, and he and Mom were both trained in hand-to-hand combat, if necessary.

They spied a yacht in the distance, and rapidly approached it. Long, white and sleek—General Puentes' yacht looked expensive. Jake wondered if it was his personal yacht, or one provided to him officially as the head of the ELLIS Forces. It looked shorter than a football field, so he guessed it was about 80 yards long—a beauty.

Pulling alongside, their own speedboat seemed tiny.

A sailor attached a portable ladder to the yacht's side, and Mom climbed up followed by Jake, Colonel Lett and Colonel Barbena. But the sailor held up a hand to stop the bodyguards.

"You're not allowed to come aboard," he warned, a hand on his pistol at his side.

Mom frowned, and Jake looked down uncertainly. In this situation, he felt naked without the Risonian military escort. He didn't trust General Puentes' motives or actions.

Mom said, "Surely you understand that we need our entourage."

That was a delicate way of putting it, Jake thought, but it didn't work.

"The General was very specific. Only you and your son have permission to come aboard."

Mom's nose scrunched in that funny Risonian way that signaled confusion. "We have permission to come aboard but not my bodyguards?"

At the word, "bodyguards" the sailor became even more rigid. "No bodyguards." His voice was cold and harsh.

Mom nodded calmly. "Very well. Lead on."

The bodyguards started to protest, but Mom held up a hand and stopped them. "We'll be back. Go eat ten sharks."

That was code. Humans knew nothing of what Risonians ate. They would wrongly assume that Mom had told the bodyguards to go eat a lunch of shark, or something equally foolish. Instead, it meant if Jake and Mom weren't out in ten minutes, they should come after them. Colonel Lett and Colonel Barbena nodded grimly and dropped back to the speedboat deck.

The sailor led the way toward the rear section of the deck, where a table and chairs were set up in the sunlight—what little there was left of it. Here in the North Sea, the winter sun set as early as 3:45 p.m. The spacious deck was protected from the winds, and was lit by strings of miniature Christmas lights that crisscrossed the ceiling in a set of artificial stars.

The General didn't rise when they came it, something that irked Jake. This wasn't going to go well, he decided. Which meant that he wanted to stay close to the deck's railings. From there, he could signal the bodyguards or escape if necessary.

Mom appeared calm, but Jake knew the subtle signals that only another Risonian would notice: the narrowed eyes, flared nostrils, and the way she held her arms out a bit to keep her gills from sweating too much. She wasn't pleased with this man's disrespect.

The deck chairs were cushioned in pale yellow. Without waiting to be asked, Mom sat in the most spacious chair, took off her windbreaker and set it beside her. Jake smiled to himself. She'd probably just taken the General's favorite chair—and she knew it.

Mom waited, calm and composed, a faint smile on her face. In other words, Jake thought, battle ready. All his senses were on high alert, too, and he found himself fidgeting with the zipper of his own windbreaker. The General went back to reading some papers. Even sitting, he towered over Mom, which meant he had to be over six feet tall. His white hair was close cropped in a military cut, except he had long sideburns. Even from across the deck, Jake smelled cigar smoke.

It was a test of wills, Jake realized, to see who would speak first. You didn't play that sort of game with Mom because she always won.

A white-garbed servant came up and offered Jake a selection of drinks. The wind in his face coming out in the speedboat had made him thirsty. Jake accepted a cup of hot tea and took a big gulp. Mom frowned at him, and immediately, he realized his error. It was a classic ploy, trying to get them to drink something that was drugged. He plunked the teacup and saucer onto the table. Closing his eyes, he tried to feel if anything was different in his body. When it all seemed normal, he opened his eyes and shrugged at his mom. Maybe it really was just an innocent cup of tea.

The servant glided silently to Mom and offered her a drink, too, but she refused to acknowledge him at all, and eventually, he left.

Finally, General Puentes stood and came from around his table. Six foot three inches, Jake decided. He wore ELLIS Forces fatigues, a casual choice that made sense. Jake bet that in a dress-uniform, the General could charm the ladies. As it was, Jake quivered inside, worried that Puentes could too easily overpower his mom.

"Let's get down to business." Puentes sat in a small yellow-cushioned chair and looked uncomfortable at its size.

Mom answered formally, "I am Ambassador Dayexi Quad-de, Consort of Swann Quad-de, Prime Minister of Tizzalura. I am at your service." It was only a fraction of her ceremonial titles, but enough for this situation.

"Yes, I know who you are," General Puentes said in a clipped voice. "And I have a request for you from the ELLIS Forces. Leave Earth. And never come back."

Jake sucked in a breath. This was harsher and more direct than he'd expected.

Mom answered in her most reasonable voice. "Where do you expect us to go?"

"I don't give a damn. Just leave Earth."

Mom grimaced, "That's a problem."

"Your problem. Not ours."

"But it is your problem," Mom said calmly. "You found us."

"No, you found us."

Mom took a deep breath and launched into her usual message: "Earth sent the Arecibo message to the far reaches of the galaxy. If we hadn't intercepted and decoded that message, things would be different. When we imploded from our own stupidity, Earth would never know that we died. But you did make first contact. You do know of our dilemma. We freely admit that it's a problem we created in a foolish attempt to control volcanoes and nature. But all Risonians will die unless we find a place for our people."

"So, an entire world will die," General Puentes said harshly. "But Earth will survive. If we let you come here—" he paused to jab a finger at Mom "—you'll destroy us, too."

Mom sat unmoving, obviously angry. "Then why did you invite my son and I here today? You said you wanted to negotiate."

"The negotiations start now." General Puentes nodded to his men, and promptly another dozen appeared from the other side of the deck. The trap had sprung.

Mom stood slowly and backed away from the General and toward Jake. If she'd been faster, they might have escaped easily. But her outrage made her slow in reacting, like she wanted to stay and argue long past the point where words would matter. In fact, Jake thought bitterly, words had never mattered. Puentes had decided everything before they arrived.

Mom lunged left, and Puentes mirrored her movement.

A half smile played across his lips, like a predator toying with its prey. But he had yet to meet a Tizzalurian backed into a corner and forced to fight. Fear crawled up Jake's spine, but he ignored it.

Bending over, Mom upended a small table, sending it crashing into the General's knees. He stumbled, off balance, and fell to one knee. Meanwhile, Mom rushed toward Jake. They met halfway and turned back to back to meet the other soldiers who had charged by now.

Mom's blade was in her right hand, and her windbreaker in her other hand to flick at attackers or to deflect attacks. Jake's matching blade dropped smoothly from the forearm brace, and he smiled grimly. He was sorry it had come to this, but not surprised.

Protecting each other's backs, they moved steadily toward the deck railings. Jake's heart pounded, hopeful but unsure. They were outnumbered and in the enemy's camp—not a strong position.

Puentes called to his troops, "I want them alive."

The soldiers bent to put their machine guns onto the deck flooring. Instead, they pulled out knives and advanced.

That was fine with Jake because it meant the soldiers wouldn't put everything they had into an attack. Mom slowly started turning so that Jake was backing up toward the deck rail and didn't have anyone to defend against. Anger blazed at her attempt to protect him, when they needed to work together.

Suddenly, a short, quick man darted in from the left and slashed at Mom's knife arm. Only Jake's strict training kept him from crying out and going to help her. But she didn't need his help. She countered with a slash of her own and ducked away. Her arm was barely scratched, just a few spots where blood drops pooled. From her expression, it had bothered Jake more than Mom.

Just as the short man danced away, a man with tattoos on his knuckles charged from the right. This time, Jake was there and met him knife blade to knife blade, the weapons making a tremendous clang. Eye to eye for a moment, Jake's street fighting lessons took over. In street fighting, anything was fair, as long as it gave you an advantage. Jake stomped down on the man's foot, and when his opponent bent double, Jake jerked his knee up to connect with the man's chin. Stumbling back, the attacker yowled loudly.

Jake was already advancing, though, trying to take advantage of the moment. He thrust, forcing the man to back up again. But he knew his place and stopped the chase. Instead, he backed up until he and Mom had each other's backs again. The Risonians were surrounded now by four or five soldiers, with more coming. The tattoo man dodged inside again, his face an angry snarl. Instead of stabbing, he kicked out, surprising Jake, and knocking his knife from his hand.

Quickly, Jake reached to the small of his back for his smaller knife and managed to lift it in time to block the tattoo man's thrust by slicing at the man's fingers.

Immediately, the tattooed man dropped his knife—and shook blood from his knuckles, but he didn't back off. He grabbed Jake's hands and twisted, forcing Jake's own knife toward his torso.

Squirming, Jake tried to twist or throw the man off balance or—but the man pushed Jake's knife downward until it was at Jake's shirt. Suddenly, the man jerked, and Jake's knife curved inward to slice a line across his belly.

Jake sucked in air, trying not to cry out with the pain. It was deep, he realized.

By now, though, they'd reached the deck railing and Jake did the only logical thing. He clambered over the railing and then held off the men as Mom scrambled over.

Puentes rushed them now, yelling, "No! Don't let them get away."

But Mom and Jake thrust away from the yacht and let themselves fall feet first into the water. It was like falling a couple of stories, and the shock of sinking might have surprised Jake if he hadn't been in the habit of rock jumping for fun. His water breathing kicked in automatically, and he looked around for Mom. She was beside him, kicking upward, and they broke the surface together. A lifeline was thrown to them from their speedboat, and within moments, Colonel Lett and Colonel Barbena had them hauled into the boat, the motor roaring to life as soon as they were heaved over the side, and they leapt away toward shore.

Jake feared a barrage of machine gun fire, but the yacht was silent. A haze of cold, stinging rain started, and Jake stood at the rear of the boat gazing at the disappearing yacht. Shaking his head, Jake wondered why he wasn't angry. Instead, sadness filled him. Earth held both rainbows and the ELLIS forces. How could it be so beautiful one moment and so ugly the next?

Mom demanded a phone and started calling people: Dad to tell officials that whatever they heard from military sources, they were fine; the NY Embassy to tell them the same thing; and then Commander Gordon of the Risonian military to demand an intensive investigation of General Puentes.

Jake wanted to tell Mom about his stomach injury, but she was so busy that he decided to go below, get the first aid kit and take it to his bunk. The bodyguards were busy with navigation and driving the boat; Mom was busy with intense discussions.

Rather than bother anyone, Jake bandaged himself. It wasn't as deep as he'd thought at first; no vital organs were hit, just a deep cut, deep enough to scar. But he was fine. Nothing to worry Mom about.

He closed his eyes, suddenly weary. Puentes and the ELLIS Forces were never going to stop fighting them. In spite of support from the political leaders of Earth, the military leaders could still stop the immigration of Risonians. Jake planted his face in his palm in despair.

THE DEBATE

December 20

Mom dropped her computer tablet onto the table and sighed. "We have another ten thousand YouTube views on the Face of Rison channel, but will it help?"

"You shouldn't check the stats every day," Jake said shortly. He sat rigid, arms casually held against the bandages on his stomach, trying to hold in the pain without letting Mom know about the injury.

"I know," she said harshly. "Just like I shouldn't read the reports from Rison on a daily basis. The number of new eruptions, the growth of the black hole in the center of our planet, the deaths—" She stopped short and passed a hand over her face. She stirred the Scottish oatmeal around in her bowl and finally took a tiny bite, frowned, and pushed the bowl away. She shoved her chair back and stood. "We leave as soon as we can get to the airport. Let's get packed."

"No."

Mom spun toward him. "What?"

"I'm not a diplomat. I've tried. David and Jillian made the trip with me, and they deserve a look around, too."

"You want to do some sight-seeing? While things fall apart?" She stood with her fists on her hips, glaring.

Jake calmly buttered an English muffin and spread orange marmalade on it. He took a big bite and chewed. Finally, when he judged that Mom's glare was about to burn a hole in him, he said, "I have to look for Em."

Mom pulled out one of the chairs drawn up to the breakfast table and sat heavily. "Her again."

"Em is here somewhere. And it's got something to do with the Phoke."

"Fairy tales!"

"Lady Zuzanna Coombe, the Lord Provost's mother said, 'Go to St. Abbs.'"

Mom tilted her head now and said thoughtfully. "Well, maybe I don't have to be in New York. Many politicians are still here in Scotland. And London would be a good base to find others to talk with."

Jake nodded and winced at the pain in his stomach. "I don't know if I want you to travel far right now. ELLIS might hijack our plane or plant a bomb on it or—"

"Oh, stop," Mom said. "We take precautions. We can't live in fear."

That was an ironic statement, Jake thought. All his life he'd lived in fear of volcanic eruptions. Fear of a hijacking or a bomb was no different.

"But," Mom continued, "we can't stay here for long. By New Year's Day, I want to be back in New York. If not before."

Jake grinned in elation. That gave him ten days to find Em. He finished his muffin and reached for another, confident that he'd already won. If Mom was thinking of alternatives, then he wouldn't have to leave right away.

But his emotions crashed when he thought about the difficulties of finding Em. He wondered if she was drinking coffee and eating Earth muffins, or if she was sick and in some hospital.

Suddenly, he wasn't hungry anymore. Shoving away his muffin, he stood and strode to stare out the window at the city of Edinburgh. She was an ancient city that held many secrets. He was so tired of secrets and searching and coming up short. He just wanted to find Em. Now.

What would make her so sick that they had to spirit her away?

He shook his head in despair. The one thing that drove him was the uncertainty. That, and the word she had scrawled on her doctor's business card: Help!

MERLIN CHARTERS

December 21

The next morning, Jake, Jillian and David piled into a small car with Colonel Barbena. She passed around lattes to the teens, who were still yawning. And she handed Jake a small package.

"It's the GPS you asked for," she said.

"Colonel, is it easy driving on the wrong side of the road?" Jillian asked.

Colonel Barbena said, "Not bad. You get used to it fast. By the way, today I'm just a chaperone, not military. Call me Hilario."

Jake rubbed sleep from his eyes and realized she wasn't dressed in her usual military uniform, but had on a warm jacket, boots and a stocking cap with a blond braid sticking out the bottom. Still, it was strange to think of her by her first name.

St. Abbs was only 75-80 kilometers (or 45-50 miles) away, an easy drive. The Scottish landscape held Jake spellbound. Rumbling hills and uneven dry-stone walls near the city gave way to spectacular views of the brilliant blue sea that sparkled under clear skies. Only an occasional white brushstroke of a cloud broke the expanse of blue above. The glimpses of the water teased the three teens, who were anxious to be out on the water—or in the water. Jake longed for cold winds, sea gulls and a wide-open sea. They wouldn't swim today, of course. Instead, they'd go out on a charter boat, as Lady Coombe had suggested. Still, they'd be on the water. And they were doing something solid to search for Em. Meanwhile, Mom, accompanied by Colonel Lett, would be consulting with politicians all day.

His stomach ached. The knife slash flamed an angry red this morning, but that was only part of the ache. Inside, desperation grew with each passing mile. If he didn't find Em soon, it would be too late. She'd been missing for over three weeks already. His grandparents on Bainbridge Island, Sir and

Easter, checked Em's house every day, but it was still empty. Phoke was their only clue.

Finally, the waters of the St. Abbs Harbor lay before them, dotted with large craggy rocks, some covered in ancient moss and others in luminous golden lichen. The stone houses with red tiled roofs and the three-story whitewashed houses with slate roofs carried a rugged charm that softened the stark winter landscape, all gray and brown. Perhaps in the summer when green lay across the undulating landscape, and glass-bottom boat tours were popular, it would be called beautiful. Now, on this clear but frigid day, it wasn't its beauty that held Jake's interest, but its strength. It was a powerful landscape, one that hinted of magic and mystery.

What was Aberforth Hills? Jake wondered. And where was it? And was Em even anywhere near Aberforth Hills? If this outing turned up nothing, he had few ideas or leads on where to turn next. He sipped his latte and wondered if he and Em would ever get back to the Blackbird Bakery on Bainbridge Island.

Hilario found parking easily. Walking down to the harbor, the wind cut sharply through their jackets. Behind them, a line of humble houses silhouetted the horizon. Before them, frothy waves broke across massive rocks before tumbling onto scoured gravel beaches. It wasn't a day for tourists.

Pushing into the tiny office of Merlin Charters, Hilario took the lead. "Hello?" she called. "Anyone here?"

From behind a short counter, an old man answered. "Aye."

"Good," Hilario answered. "We have a charter reservation for the day."

"T'will be cold on the water. Are ye that sure now that you want to be going out?"

"Aye," Jake answered, mimicking the man's Scottish accent. "The Lady Zuzanna Coombe sent us to you. Her grandmother lived here in St. Abbs, I believe."

"Aye." The man wore a heavy, dark polished-cotton jacket and loose waterproof pants. "Her mother would be Freya Watley, a fine woman, gone these ten years."

Jake nodded. "Mrs. Watley told her daughter stories of Aberforth Hills. That's what we'd like to see today."

The man fingered his white beard and blinked dark eyes at them. "Ye've come to chase a myth? For that's all it tis, a story."

Jillian snapped a couple photos of the old man. "What's your name? Can I take your photo? Will you tell us the story of Aberforth Hills?" She jabbed at her phone, obviously uploading the photos to some social media or other. The photo of the old Scottish sailor would be popular on her accounts.

"I'm Captain Crow. Sure, and I don't care if ye take my photo. And no, I won't repeat a story that's just a myth." He picked up a fishing net and starting spreading it out for inspection. "I'll tell ye again. There's nothing but water to see, and t'will be a cold day on the seas. Ye really don't want to go out."

David stepped forward now. "Sir, we're Americans from Seattle, Washington, which is on the Pacific Ocean, so we're used to cold days on the water. Seattle is far enough north that your town feels familiar. We're not looking for anything sensational, just doing some sightseeing. Regardless of any story you tell us or don't tell us, we want to go out on the water. But if a story would make it more—" he waved a hand "—I don't know. If it would make the trip more magical, well, that's all we're looking for."

What was it about David that made his request seem so reasonable and peaceful? Jake wondered. Because the old man's face softened.

"Well, sightseeing, we can do that. Aye," said Captain Crow. Suddenly, he smiled. "Sure, and I'll take ye to see Aberforth Hills."

Jake stared at his dimpled cheeks. He got the impression there was a private joke here somewhere, but without something solid to base that feeling on, there was nothing to do but smile and agree. After all, they were getting what they wanted.

Captain Crow's boat was old, but in excellent shape. Stepping aboard the Captain patted the deck rails affectionately.

"Gretchen?" Jillian asked, snapping a photo of the boat's name. "Was there a real Gretchen?"

Captain Crow's face sagged under his cap. "My wife. Gone these twenty years."

Jillian said, "Do you have children?"

Apparently, though, the Captain was finished with small talk. He went to work checking his motor and generally bustling around doing things that Jake didn't understand. In the end, the motor purred.

Crow was used to tourist work and made sure his guests were comfortably seated behind a glass pane that kept the worst of the wind off them. He piled blankets on a seat and said, "Use what ye like."

Jillian and Hilario sat with their back to the wind, snuggled under several thick blankets. Hilario casually stretched out her legs and draped a blanket over them for show. But Jillian honestly just liked the snuggling, in spite of her magma-sapiens blood. Even David took a blanket, but he set it beside himself and sat looking forward, not back.

It seemed only Jake was hot. He unbuttoned his jacket and sat at the back of the boat away from the glass screen.

"Anyone get seasickness?" Captain Crow asked.

That brought smiles from all of them. David answered for them, "We're pretty comfortable on the water."

"Then let's go see Aberforth Hills." Captain Crow cast off the lines, and then steered the boat out into the open water of the harbor.

Jake was beginning to wonder if Captain Crow's dimples came with a strange sense of humor. He refused to talk while piloting the boat, but ever so often, he looked over at the teens and broke into a full smile, complete with the dimples. Like he was enjoying some joke, but he was the only one who knew the punch line.

Meanwhile, Jake got busy with his technology. First, he made sure the GPS app on his smart phone was on and working, and then he stashed the phone in an inside pocket where he wouldn't be tempted to keep looking at it. Instead, he asked the Captain if he had a pocketknife and cut open the hard plastic of a package. He handed the knife back to Captain Crow, who asked, "What's that?"

"GPS," Jake said.

Captain Crow dipped his head and looked away toward the horizon.

Jake spread out the setup instructions and started setting the time, date and other settings until it was working, and he had a GPS reading.

Looking up, he realized they were far out to sea now, with land a distant horizon.

"How much farther?" he asked.

Shrugging, Captain Crow said, "To find a myth? We could go forever." But he kept motoring anyway. Apparently, he had some destination in mind.

Even in the full wind, Jake was hot. His stomach wound itched, but it hurt to scratch. Up front, David and Jillian were chatting, while Hilario seemed to be napping. Maybe Jake should've told Mom about the wound. But there were no Risonian doctors here, and really, what could she do but wait and see if it healed on its own? He'd saved her a worry she didn't need after the Puentes disaster. Still, it was starting to worry Jake. Risonians rarely ever ran a temperature like humans because their body temperatures were already hotter. But he didn't feel so good.

Without warning, the boat slowed and stopped. The waves here were gentle, so the boat just rocked.

"I'll get our lunch," Captain Crow said. "And then, we'll talk."

Again, the Captain proved to be experienced in dealing with tourists. He poured steaming tea from a huge thermos, and then handed around sausage sandwiches on hand-made rolls. A giant tin of shortbread—the Scottish did know how to make shortbread!—completed the simple meal. But on the water, the simple fare was a treat.

And then, he talked.

"I'll tell ye the tale of Aberforth Hills," Captain Crow began. "Once long, long ago, the Mer folk lived only in the warm seas, like the Mediterranean. Slowly, though, some of the Mer took to land, and of course, they became fishermen and expert in the ways of boats. And by and by, they came to the North Sea. Here, they found amber. Do you know of amber?"

"Yes," David said. "We stopped at a jewelry store yesterday, and they told us how it was made, and why the North Sea has so much of it.

59

Captain Crow nodded and continued, "Soon they began trading the baubles at various ports. A rich trade quickly grew up around the harvesting and sale of amber. If the stories of Aberforth Hills are true, then it was amber that brought the Mer folk here."

"The Phoke," Jillian corrected.

"Pah!" exploded Captain Cross. "They are the Mer, not the Phoke. Why would ye use some Greek word for Scottish mermen and mermaids?"

"It's an updated name." Jillian shrugged. "For the 21st century."

Captain Cross waved a hand dismissing the whole younger generation. "Anyway, the Mer built Aberforth Hills as the center of amber trade. Made them rich."

Even if it was a story, Jake found it encouraging that the water folk had found something valued by the humans to trade. They'd found their economic niche in the human world. If—no, when—the Risonians were allowed to come to Earth, they'd face similar problems of how to earn a living. They'd need to figure out what jobs they could do better than humans and then figure out how to do them for a profit.

"Is Aberforth Hills still there? Under us right now?" Jake asked softly.

Captain Crow threw back his head and laughed, a deep belly laugh. "It's a story, boy. A myth."

Jake didn't like being laughed at, but really, what had he expected? They were in the middle of the North Sea, at some random place probably. There was no Aberforth Hills.

But then, where was Em? It was an ache in his gut that he couldn't quiet.

"What's the water depth here?" David asked.

Captain Crow looked at his gauges and answered, "About 90 meters. 89.3. 90.2. The readings vary as we drift."

Jake mentally translated that to American measurements: roughly 270 feet deep.

Peering over the boat's side, David asked. "Could we figure out if there are seven hills under us?"

"Aye. If ye had the time and the gas to do it. Ye'd need to drive a grid across this empty ocean and track the depth."

Hilario leaned forward now. "There are depth charts of the seas, right?"

Captain Crow shrugged. "Aye. In shipping lanes, especially. But in reality, we've only mapped maybe 10% of the sea floors. Here?" He nodded toward the water. "No one has mapped the whole of the North Sea. There could be dozens of hills. For that matter, what's your definition of a hill? A hill might be something that's 100 meters taller than the sea floor. Or does 50 meters make it a hill?"

Jake felt disgruntled. He'd paid to see Aberforth Hills. Instead, there was just the open sea and pointless questions.

Something was suspicious, though. There was a certain bravado about the captain, like he's just pulled a good joke on this American kid.

What if—despite everything—Captain Crow had indeed brought them to Aberforth Hills? What if it was right underneath them as they spoke? The irony of the possibility made Jake cringe.

He consulted his new GPS unit and saved the current readings. He must find a way to return to this point and go swimming. Hilario and Mom wouldn't allow it, probably. Or maybe it was close enough to shore that he could swim out some night. With his legs Velcroed, he was a fast swimmer—and the nights were long this time of year. Would David and Jillian go for the idea?

Hilario looked at him now and asked, "Are you OK? Your face is red."

Jake frowned and said, "Just hot."

"Hot?" Captain Crow asked in surprise. "It's cold out here, and ye've been sitting in the wind."

"We're stopped. The wind isn't bad now," Jake said grumpily.

Hilario threw off her blanket, stepped to his side, and laid a hand first on his forehead and then on his cheek. "You are hot." Her eyebrows drew together in confusion. "Why?"

Jake waved a hand. "Nothing."

"Why?" she demanded more vehemently.

Jake hesitated. His stomach wound was hurting even more now. Maybe he should let her look.

Just then, a large wave heaved the boat upward. Thrown off balance, Captain Crow fell heavily onto Jake, knocking the GPS unit from his hands. Jake watched it sail over the side of the boat and disappear into the depths. Hilario hauled the Captain off Jake and shoved him to the opposite side of the deck. With a wide-legged stance for balance, she stood with her arms up like she was ready to fight.

Jake stood and put a hand on her shoulder to let her know that he was all right. He glared at the Captain. "Why'd you do that? That GPS was brand new."

"The wave knocked me off balance." His voice was calm, almost reassuring.

For a moment, they stared each other down, but the old man gave in first. He shrugged, went back to the motor, and started it. Hilario shrugged, but sat beside Jake just in case. The boat turned and headed back to shore.

Hilario started to say something about Jake's temperature, but he shook his head. "When we get back to shore."

Hilario frowned, but that's all she'd get while they were with someone else, Jake thought. He wouldn't show her anything until they had privacy.

Still sitting in the wind at the back of the boat, Jake watched the old sea captain work. It could be a coincidence, he thought. The GPS unit had been a sort of test. Would Captain Crow let him mark the spot? Or would he do something to make sure they didn't return to that exact, nondescript spot on the sea? Maybe the wave had been an accident. But Captain Crow didn't seem like the casual sort of seaman to let a small wave knock him off balance.

Either way, Jake still had the GPS app on his smart phone. He would return to that spot and see what lay under the waves.

A TOUR OF ABERFORTH HILLS

December 21

"My dad is a Captain in the Aberforth Hills militia. He sent me over to show you the city." Shelby Bulmer, the nurse's aide held Em's arm to lend her support, even though Em was much stronger today. She had been allowed to dress in jeans, t-shirt and tennis shoes. He wore loose-fitting hospital scrubs.

"Why does he want me to see the city?" Em asked. She was studying Shelby carefully, trying to see what made him a Mer instead of a human. His hair, ears, hands, arms, legs—everything looked normal to her.

Shelby had blond hair and a Nordic look. She also guessed that he did some body-building because his arms were so muscled. If she got too tired on this city tour, she was confident that he could carry her back to the hospital. He said, "They want you to go to school here."

Startled, Em shook her head. "I won't. I'm already winning swim meets, and by my senior year, I'll swim well enough to get college scholarships."

"We have swim meets, too."

"Where? Underwater? You swim against the sharks or something?"

"Aberforth Hills is going to be a surprise to you," he said with amusement.

He opened a door, and Em stopped in alarm. The building's spacious hallway was connected to a tunnel with a low ceiling that couldn't have been seven feet tall at best. It was wide enough for ten people or more to pass at a time. It smelled damp, like a musty bathroom. Not any worse than an old subway in a major city, she guessed, but she didn't like it.

"Most buildings these days are connected by tubes." Shelby didn't notice her unease, but he kept walking and gently drawing her forward.

Suddenly, a hover-car darted around a corner and rushed straight for them. Quickly, Em stepped to the side of the corridor and pulled in to avoid being hit. Instead, it smoothly stopped right beside them. About the size of a golf cart, it rode on air somehow and made almost no noise as it moved.

A man and woman wearing white coats—just like doctors in any hospital—stepped out. The man said, "Would you like this h-car? We're done for now."

"Thanks," Shelby said. He climbed in and motioned for Em to sit. Pulling a lever, he smoothly turned it around, and they shot off down the tubes. He explained, "We have a couple thousand h-cars in the tubes. Usually you leave them at a tube station, but for the hospital, you can take them to the entrance, if you need to. I usually find an abandoned one here when I get off work."

They came into a larger tube, and Em realized they'd been in a small branch of the tube system. The larger thoroughfares would easily hold twenty or thirty people across, were taller and much cleaner. There were three lanes: two for h-cars, one for each travel direction, and one for pedestrians. At the next major intersection, Shelby stopped to show her a tube station. A row of h-cars sat in haphazard rows; a mother pulled a toddler into one and zipped off to the right, while another car stopped and a man in a business suit got off, grabbed a briefcase, and strode briskly away.

"Every tube station has a moon pool," Shelby said. "And an O2 Station."

He explained that before a dive, the Mer often breathed straight oxygen to enable them to stay underwater longer. They needed that extra oxygen to reach the surface easily from this depth.

Watching the traffic come and go, Em saw a sign that said, Phelps Natatorium.

"Wait!" Em said astonished. "Phelps? Michael Phelps?"

"Think about it." Shelby just raised an eyebrow and waited for her to understand.

"Oh!" The incredulous truth hit her, and she thought about how unfair that was for humans. But, wow! Phelps.

Shelby just grinned. "Aberforth Hills has lots of surprises for you."

"Can I see the Natatorium?" Em was anxious to see something familiar in this alien place.

"The Natatorium is at the northern edge of the city. It's too far for you to go today. I'm only allowed to give you a short outing so you don't get tired," Shelby said. "What else do you want to see?"

What Em really yearned for was to know more about her biological mother, Bobbie Fleming. Ms. Fleming been in Seattle High School her junior year, but her brother thought she was getting too interested in human boys. He pulled her back to Aberforth Hills for her senior year. But then, thinking she was "cured" of that boy-craze and back in control, she attended Seattle Pacific University. And as a sophomore, she met Damien Fleming again.

Em wanted to know where her mother had lived that senior year. To see it. To walk through it. To try to understand why Ms. Fleming had given Em up for adoption. Was it possible to understand a decision like that?

Em answered slowly. "Bobbie Fleming is my mother." She winced. It felt wrong to say that, like she was betraying her Mom. Hastily, she added, "My biological mother. Do you think we could go places where she grew up?" She wondered what would it be like to grow up in a hidden society and to pledge to keep that society going. What would that do to your psyche?

"Sure," Shelby said. "Your Uncle Max wants you to stay at the family house tonight anyway and that's in the eastern part of the city. Someone is taking your clothes and things there, and we'll meet him for supper."

Em shook her head in annoyance. How dare Dr. Max Bari just take over her life like that! Well, she didn't plan to be here long. She'd be back on Bainbridge Island soon and everything would be back to normal. No, she thought, life will never be the same again. Knowing who gave me life and seeing this place with my own eyes—everything has changed.

And anyway, she wanted to see Bobbie's school. And she was well enough to be out of the hospital, and where else could she stay until she was well enough to travel.

"OK," she said with a deep sigh. "Where else could we go to see something about Bobbie?"

Em didn't know what she expected. After all, what did Shelby know about her biological mother? But he managed to find the right information. First, they stopped by the Gunby High School and walked down a hallway that looked very much like any school building anywhere on Earth.

Em sat on a wooden bench while Shelby ducked into the school's office to let them know he was touring the building with Em. Looking around, she saw no windows, and everything smelled faintly of mildew.

When Shelby reappeared, she asked, "What's that smell?"

Shelby wrinkled his nose. "The school has one of the oldest air generators around. It's so old that the air it produces smells funny. I don't even notice it, I'm so used to it."

Shelby led the way up a set of stairs and to a wall with photos.

"Whoa!" Shelby said. "Look at those hair styles."

The senior photo of Bobbie Fleming—or Bobbie Bari, her maiden name—showed a pretty girl with big hair like the models of the time with feathered bangs and layers to make her hair look fuller. Em's heart twisted to see Bobbie so young and happy. This was the woman that Damien Fleming had fallen in love with.

Em touched the glass in front of Bobbie's photo. They didn't look alike at all. Apparently Em had gotten her father's coloring not her mom's. She suddenly realized that she didn't know why Bobbie Fleming had been a patient in the Mangot Hospital. There had been such startling things to discuss that she hadn't even thought to ask. Hopefully, it wasn't something serious. She started to ask, but didn't think Shelby would have any idea.

Shelby stopped at the school library, and Em gratefully sank into a chair beside a study table. While she rested, he talked to the librarian and found a school year book. Bringing it back to Em's table, they looked up Bobbie Bari.

"Looks like she played tennis. And she played Juliet in the senior play," he said. "We can look at those buildings, too."

Emotions flickered, leaving Em alternately hot and cold, angry and sympathetic. Desperately, she tried to understand what it was like for Ms. Fleming as a teenager. Living the secret life of a mermaid, but longing to be just a normal American teenager—it would have been bewildering. Interesting that they studied Shakespeare's love story. Star-crossed lovers.

Em realized she was tired, not just a usual weariness, but a deep exhaustion from her illness. The thought of going to Dr. Bari's house, though, repelled her. Not yet.

"Let's see something else," she said. Resolutely, she rose and walked briskly, trying to hide her fatigue.

In the h-car again, Em asked, "Ms. Fleming played tennis?"

"Yes, we'll go to the Wolliscroft Tennis Club in the eastern part of the city. It was actually established in 1868, the same year as the All England Club in Wimbledon. Of course, we didn't really have a tennis facility here until about twenty years ago, but just the same, the Phoke stuck together and pushed hard to win a couple Wimbledons."

Em thought: *Of course, you did. You push hard about everything.*

She was starting to realize at least that much about the Phoke.

"For the last twenty-five years," Shelby continued, "we've held our own tennis tournaments. Your mother won the girls event her senior year. In those days, we weren't very good at tennis, but nowadays, we've built to a level that it's not uncommon for our players to compete on a world level." The pride in his voice was obvious.

The Wolliscroft Tennis Club was beautiful. A pale silvery metal exterior hid a perfectly heated and cooled space with a series of courts, dressing rooms, small vendors with snacks, and tennis equipment. The center courts could easily hold 3-4000 spectators. Everywhere, people waved at Shelby or called to him. Apparently, he was well known in the tennis world.

"Who pays for all of this?" Em asked incredulously.

"The Mer made our fortunes in the amber trade." He explained the underwater origins of the stone and some history of its trade. "But our businessmen have a hand in almost everything these days."

He sounded so superior that Em wanted to knock him down a couple notches. "If I wasn't so sick," she said, "I'd challenge you to a swim race."

"You'd win," he said seriously. "I'm only one-fourth Mer, too, but you've had training. But I'm more keen on tennis than swimming. And on bodybuilding. If you want a race, you should challenge someone who's half Mer. You'll likely lose, even with all your practice."

"It makes that much difference?"

He shrugged and said simply, "Michael Phelps."

Em struggled to understand, but she felt like she'd been left behind in an algebra class while the rest of the class had jumped to calculus. She also felt like it was the end of a very, very long school day.

She was glad when Shelby finally said, "Well, it's time to meet your Uncle for dinner."

Even in her fatigue, Em felt a deep resolve stiffen inside her. This tour of Aberforth Hills had her blood running cold. Uncle. Doctor. Horrible brother. Half Mer, and too proud of it. Dr. Max Bari was going to try to control her life. Aberforth Hills enticed her as he knew it would; it was exotic and intriguing. But Em wouldn't let him bully her like he had Bobbie Fleming. She couldn't stay here. She needed to return to Bainbridge Island as soon as possible. Before she forgot that she was half-Japanese and all-American.

NIGHT SWIMMING

December 21

To spend the night, Hilario Barbena had rented a small, whitewashed three-bedroom cottage on Coldingham Bay, just south of St. Abbs. It was charmingly decorated with photos of surfers and kite surfers—obviously a popular summer pastime here. The two boys shared a room; Jillian and Hilario each had their own rooms.

They stopped at a local shop and bought hamburger meat, the teens all tired of Scottish food and longing for a familiar cheeseburger. Jake added a bottle of antiseptic and bandages to the basket, and at Hilario's glare, said he'd show her when they got to the house.

At the cabin, David volunteered to grill the burgers. He lit the gas grill outside, shaped the meat into patties, and carried them out to cook.

Meanwhile, Hilario demanded, "Let me see."

Jake pulled off his shirt and heard a sharp intake of air from both Hilario and Jillian.

He quickly explained how he'd been cut by General Puentes's men.

In a tight, angry voice, Hilario said, "You didn't tell your mother? It's definitely infected."

Jake shrugged. "Why worry her?"

"Turn this way to the light, so I can get a pic," Jillian said, her smart phone in her hands.

"No," Jake said. "This isn't for your adoring public."

"Aw," Jillian said. "They'd love to see how an alien hurts."

"Yeah," Jake said cynically. "I'm sure they would. But go find another alien for that task."

Jillian frowned. "You're really sick?" She put a hand on his forehead and nodded. "You ARE really sick! When's the last time you ever ran a fever?"

"Um, never," Jake said. They couldn't use a human's thermometer to take his temperature; Risonian body temperatures ran hot anyway, with 108 degrees Fahrenheit a normal reading. No human thermometer was made to measure that, and

Hilario's tiny Risonian first-aid kit didn't have a Risonian thermometer because it was needed so rarely.

Hilario rummaged in the kitchen and found some acetaminophen left by a previous renter. She shook out a couple white pills and handed them to Jake. "I'm not sure this will work on Rison physiology. If you get worse, we'll have to find a doctor."

David came back in with the grilled burgers and caught the end of that conversation. Even sick, Jake was ready for cheeseburgers, potato chips, pickles and chocolate chip cookies. Much better than haggis, he thought wryly.

After supper, Hilario and Jillian cleaned up the kitchen. Jake was sick, and David had done the cooking, so they volunteered. Meanwhile, Jake pulled out his smart phone and opened the GPS app. He and David bent over the phone, trying to figure out the app.

David finally said, "We've got the coordinates. We can find it again."

"When?" Jillian asked.

"Now," Jake said.

Hilario sighed. "You're right. We should swim out tonight and see if there's anything there. It'll be a fast swim, with little time to investigate. But we should be able to find out if we need to go back when we have more time."

Jillian nodded to Jake, "Do you feel up to it? How bad do you feel?"

"The cold water will actually help my temperature go down." His forehead furrowed. "I have enough energy to make it."

David nodded to the window. "Five o'clock but already dark. We can go now, and no one will see us."

Hilario said, "You three stay here. I'll go buy a waterproof GPS."

By 6 p.m., the four stood at the water's edge on the small sandy Coldingham Bay beach. Hilario held a waterproof GPS that had a lighted display screen. She'd be the lead swimmer and navigator. She handed around waterproof flashlights, too.

Jake strapped his light to his forehead and grinned at Jillian who was already shaking her head to play with her light. But there was no sense in playing around. They had serious business to attend to.

Jake murmured, "Aberforth Hills, here we come." And they dove into the night sea.

Cold and clear, the water here was a pleasure. No silt like they might have found where a stream emptied into the North Sea. Almost immediately a seal swam under them and was joined by several more. With their legs zipped into an efficient tail, the Risonians easily kept pace with the seals. The seals didn't come close, just shadowed the small group of aliens as they swam.

Quickly, Jake realized he was feeling worse than he had suspected. Even with his magma-sapiens blood, the cold water made him shiver. Only his constant movement kept his teeth from chattering. He was definitely running a temperature, maybe 111 degrees or more.

But he swam. Em was hidden somewhere in Scotland, and his time was running out. If he didn't find her soon, he'd have to return to Seattle without her. He was sure that the answers were here somewhere, if he could understand the clues he saw and heard.

Gradually, Jake felt himself slowing. Hilario was still in the lead, with David right after. Jillian seesawed between speed and sympathy. She sped up to catch Hilario, and then turned around to see Jake far behind. She motioned the other two ahead and waited for Jake to catch up. Then she sped up again, only to wind up waiting for Jake again. He thrust his leg-tail harder, trying to find a comfortable way to speed up, but everything used his stomach muscles, and the cut burned, a pain that was spreading.

Still, he wouldn't give up. He kept swimming, trying to keep his eyes open and focus on Jillian's light so he wouldn't fall behind too far. Once, he found himself drifting, half asleep, and jerked his eyes open. In the distance, he saw Jillian's single light, Hilario and David too far ahead to even spot their lights.

That time, when he caught up, he motioned to Jillian to take a short break. They could talk underwater because it didn't bother them if water got into their lungs. Their lungs could eject water, in a sort of strange, forceful burp. However, water carried voices with less efficiency than air, and they sounded like they were whispering. The Old Speech, spoken before Risonians starting living on land, was a series of squeaks and whistles, a very different sort of language. Most families still taught it to their children, but they rarely spoke it in the cities on land. Only those who lived in underwater cities were proficient. The Ambassador had forbidden Risonians in the Earth delegation to speak it, lest some Earthling try to decipher it. They used it only in emergency communications, and then only on secure channels.

Jake let his body droop to say that he was tired.

Hilario and David had circled back now, concern written on their faces.

But Jake pointed to the GPS and raised an eyebrow in an unvoiced question "How much farther?"

Hilario pointed to the readout. They were very close to the spot they had marked from the day's cruise. Hilario held up ten fingers. She was estimating maybe ten minutes.

Jake nodded and doggedly kicked away, managing to briefly stay in the lead until he felt his energy drain away again, and he slowed. Now Hilario pushed hard, racing far ahead, but mimicking Jillian by waiting until Jake caught up before she darted away again.

Finally, the GPS told them that they were close to the spot where Captain Crow had taken them.

And nothing had prepared them for the sight.

RISONIAN FEVER

December 21

The Risonian aliens treaded water, staring at the sight before them. They were 90 meters deep, so any light created here wouldn't reach to the surface. Before them lay a city. No other word could describe the collection of buildings that were definitely meant for human-like creatures to live in.

Structures were obviously of various ages. The oldest—covered with barnacles and pitted from years of sea water—were like an upside-down bell. None of the older buildings had windows, presumably because of the difficulties of making glass thick enough to withstand the water pressure at this depth. The newer buildings were much like a skyscraper with five or six stories—though a "skyscraper" was a strange misnomer in this underwater city. Some of these taller building had windows, but they were small and few in number.

This was definitely an old city. Though Jake couldn't count seven hills, there were enough high points and valleys that he was confident that when he had time to swim around the city and count, there would be seven hills.

He was confused; as far as he knew, the Risonians were the only ones who were capable of building a city like this. But the buildings looked really old. Could this be a really old Seastead? Or were the tales of mermaids and mermen real? This was Aberforth Hills, of course. But that brought him no closer to an answer; it only raised more questions.

Em had to be here, in one of these buildings. Jake felt a surge of anger at whomever had taken her. He would get her back. And if he found out that the Phoke were really Risonian, he'd be furious at his mother. If there were other Risonian Seasteads, and she hadn't told him. . .

But his energy was flagging. He had to rest. Reluctantly, he tapped Hilario's shoulder. She whirled and her expression immediately went tense.

Jake jerked his head back toward shore to say he wanted to go back.

She automatically reached for his forehead and jerked back in concern. Hilario shook her hand as if it had just been burned, and the others nodded their understanding. David and Jillian each grabbed one of Jake's arms, and they pulled him through the water. Toward the end of the journey, he dozed, letting them take him where they would. He vaguely remembered stumbling into the rented cottage and Hilario talking quietly into a phone: "Ambassador, you've got to find Jake a doctor."

≈ ≈ ≈

December 22

The Emergency Room rustled with the sighs of impatient people with various medical complaints and their anxious families. Overlaid across the sound of suffering was a loud news program broadcast from three separate TVs. They hung from the ceiling and pointed in different directions so that no one in the waiting room could escape the solemn proclamations. The 6 a.m. weather program was predicting cold, but sunny weather for Christmas Day.

Jake was drawn, though, to a large wall that contained a huge salt-water aquarium. While Mom talked to officials to sort out paperwork and such, Jake tapped his forefinger on the thick glass to attract the attention of a yellow-finned fish.

"Stop that." A woman—tall, straight-backed, and almost regal—peered around the corner of the fish tank. She had the tone of one who expected to be obeyed.

"Sorry," Jake said immediately. He took a half-step back and watched.

Using a long-armed brush, the woman scoured away a speck of algae, or something, that had stuck to the aquarium's wall. She moved methodically around the tank, concentrating on eradicating every tinge of algae. She was tall and wore a navy t-shirt with the hospital logo on a front pocket, jeans and an all-weather jacket. Her dark hair was gathered into a huge knot at the nape of her neck. Jake supposed the hospital hired her to take care of the aquarium.

He said, "I went to the Scotland National Aquarium a couple days ago."

She looked up, apparently surprised at this sudden conversation. She nodded and returned to her work.

A quick glance told Jake that Mom was still filling out the emergency room papers. He studied the colorful fish in the tank and said, "They had an octopus. I met her."

"Met her?" The aquarium lady paused.

"They let me put my arm in her tank."

Now Jake had the lady's attention. She shook water off the brush and took a step closer.

"Really. What did the octopus do?"

Jake laughed, but he immediately regretted it because it made his stomach hurt. "She didn't like me. Squirted me with really cold water and then hid. They say sea creatures like to hide in plain sight. Is there something in this aquarium that I should see, but it's hidden in plain sight?"

After another long moment of silence, the woman stepped back to the aquarium, stuck the brush back in the water and started scrubbing off a new fleck of algae.

"Well?" Jake prompted.

Without turning, the woman said, "I believe it was Leonardo da Vinci who said, 'Learn how to see. Realize that everything connects to everything else.' Perhaps you just need to learn how to see?"

Jake sighed in exasperation, and started to reply, but his mother touched his shoulder. "This way," she said.

Jake shrugged at the woman and turned to follow his mother. They went through a set of double doors to a small room, where they waited again. Nurses came in to poke and prod: they checked his pulse and shook their heads over alien anatomy. They marveled over the Risonian thermometer that Mom had brought. It showed Jake's temperature at 110.5 degrees, two and a half degrees above his normal temperature of 108.

"A human would be dead at that temperature," a tiny nurse said. She wrote the temperature on a chart and stepped outside the door calling to another nurse walking by, "You won't believe this."

Mom sighed heavily with frustration. Jake realized that this was calling attention to the Risonian anatomy just at a time when they needed to look and act human. There couldn't be a worse time for him to need a doctor.

The door opened and a woman walked in, head down, studying a digital tablet. Looking up, she smiled at Jake. Startled, he realized it was the aquarium woman.

She reached out a hand to Mom, "Hello, I'm Dr. Mangot. Blake Rose asked me to stop in and see about your son. We were in medical school together."

She was his doctor! Irritated, Jake thought about her comment, "Learn to see." He'd seen what he expected to see, a person who cleaned aquariums, not a doctor.

"What seems to be the matter?" asked Dr. Mangot.

When Jake pulled up his t-shirt, she whistled. "Infected. How'd you get that cut?"

As agreed beforehand, Jake said, "Knife accident. Just playing around. Just a fluke."

"Hmmm." Clearly Dr. Mangot wasn't convinced by his comment. She sat on a rolling stool, pulled on rubber gloves, and snapped them into place. Gingerly, she touched the wound. "Does that hurt?"

Jake winced at the sharp pain and yelped, "Yes!"

Dr. Mangot rolled back and pulled off the gloves. "I'll need to do some blood work."

Mom protested. "You don't know what Risonian blood is supposed to look like."

The doctor's face was suddenly wreathed in a huge smile. "I know. Isn't it great? You don't know what an opportunity this is for a comparative anatomy specialist like myself. Blake knew. That's why he called me. And while I may not understand everything I see under a microscope, if there's Earth bacteria, I will be able to see it and understand that much."

Carefully, Mom said, "All right. How long will it take? He's running quite a high temperature."

"That's what I understand," Dr. Mangot said. "I'll draw his blood myself and try to be back within an hour. You do understand, though, that I may not be able to help if he's got an Earth bacterial infection, and I try to treat him with antibiotics. From what I know, the Risonian metabolism works much faster than ours, so he could feel fine overnight. However, I must say, human antibiotics may not work with his anatomy."

Mom nodded, "I understand. I just don't have another good choice. It'll take a couple days for one of our doctors to get here."

Dr. Mangot nodded briskly, turned to the cabinet of supplies, and pulled out a syringe and vial to hold the blood. At Jake's dismayed expression, she grinned again and said, "This won't hurt a bit."

∿ ∿ ∿

Jake huddled under the covers and tried to stop shivering. "Why didn't you tell me that we had another Seastead in the North Sea?" he asked his mother.

The question had hovered there all day while they went to the emergency room, waited for the blood tests and received a prescription. But Jake had known better than to discuss it in public places. Now that they were back in their hotel room, though, he wanted answers.

Mom, sitting in a straight-back chair beside his bed, just shook her head. Her usually curly hair was limp, and her eyes sagged from fatigue and worry. "I didn't tell you because we don't have a Seastead in the North Sea."

"It was there, Mom. And an old Seastead at that. How long have we been on Earth? Since the very first?"

"It's not ours," Mom said.

"Where else do we have Seasteads?" he said through gritted teeth. Why couldn't they just trust him and treat him like an adult? He glared at her, daring her to lie to him.

Calmly, she said, "One in the Mediterranean and one in the Atlantic."

Jake's mouth fell open. "Oh."

Mom nodded, "Yes. Oh."

"But not in the North Sea?"

She shook her head.

Jake shivered and readjusted the blankets to cover his head. "Then, whose?"

Mom's mouth thinned in frustration. "I don't know, but we've got to find out. Who else is living in Earth's seas? Our evacuation from Rison only works if the Earthlings don't care about their oceans. No," she caught herself immediately.

"They care. Some of them deeply. But they don't live there, so the connection is different than if we were asking to share their lands."

"I've been hearing stories about the Mer, a race that lives in the ocean. Or sometimes they call it the Phoke," Jake shrugged. "But everyone understands that it's just a myth."

Suddenly, there was a knock at the hotel room door.

Mom came back a few moments later. "The pharmacy sent up the antibiotic. And it's time for more acetaminophen for that fever." She handed him a large pink pill, several more acetaminophen, and half a glass of water.

Jake took the pills, drank all the water, and handed the glass back to Mom. "We've got to get back out to St. Abbs and Aberforth Hills. Whatever is there, it's my only chance of finding Em."

"If you're feeling better tomorrow, you have to dive with me. I've talked with many of the world's leaders by now, and they are scared of us. They want to know how we move and operate in the seas. We've got to dive with some of their military, the Army people."

"Navy or Marines," Jake said automatically. From his time on the Obama Moon Base, he knew better than to mix up the branches of the military.

"Officers from different branches of military and from different countries.

He sighed, "Okay. But the day after that, it's Aberforth Hills and Em."

"Fine," Mom agreed. "Now get some sleep and feel better."

UNCLE AND NIECE

December 22

When Em walked into the dining room, Dr. Bari had his back to her choosing items from a tray.

"Good evening," she said coolly.

Dr. Bari turned and gaped, visibly shocked. Shaking his head, he said, "If you had blond hair, you'd be your mother at eighteen."

Em smiled grimly. She'd slept in her mother's old room, and when the alarm woke her from her nap, she'd rummaged through the closet of outdated clothing until she'd found something reasonable: a pair of jeans, a cream-colored fisherman's sweater and tennis shoes. The surprise was that they fit, as if made for her.

"See? Even your smile is like Bobbie."

Shyly, Em said, "I'm still trying to get used to the thought that she's my biological mother."

"Yes," Dr. Bari said. "I can see that. Would you like to call me Uncle Max?"

Em was taken aback. "You're Dr. Bari," she said decisively. She didn't think she could ever think of him as family. Her family was Mom, Dad and Marisa. He was trying to butt in where he wasn't wanted. Anger stirred in her, but she forced herself to stay calm. It took too much energy to be angry.

With a nod, Dr. Bari handed her a glass of orange juice and gestured toward the buffet. It was laid with a tray of lunchmeats, cheeses and croissants to make sandwiches.

"You'll have to come to terms with the Phoke sometime, you know," Dr. Bari said. "You'll always be between your genetics and your upbringing."

"The nature versus nurture question?" she taunted. "And of course, I must choose nature."

Dr. Bari shook his head. "No, it's just that it's a classic question. And you'll have to answer it sometime." He sat at the table, bit into his sandwich, and watched her fix her lunch.

Em laid a slice of ham and then cheddar cheese onto her croissant, taking her time so she could think. She thought about how hard it was to fit in when you were so obviously different. It's not like Em was the only half-Japanese kid in their school. In first grade, there were six. Four Asian boys and two half-Asian girls. Aimi and Em. Best friends forever. Or at least for first, second, third, and fourth grades. Then Aimi's parents divorced.

Captain Ragnor Skerry, or Uncle Skerry to Em, was military, and when he moved to D.C., Aimi and her Mom didn't move with him.

Aimi was spending the night when she told Em. They were playing with Barbie and Ken. Suddenly, Aimi moved Barbie's leg to kick Ken.

Em stared in surprise. "Why'd you do that?"

"Cuz sometimes grown-ups do that. Mom doesn't love Daddy any more. She wants to go home to Japan."

Em, who adored Uncle Skerry, was shocked. "Why doesn't she love him?"

Aimi shrugged. "I don't know. She won't say anything else." Again, Barbie kicked Ken. Aimi let the Ken doll fall to the ground and said, "Let's do something else."

Em stretched out on her stomach on the turquoise rug and propped her head on her hands. Staring at Aimi, she asked, "Did your Mom really kick your Dad?"

"No. There's no hitting. They just don't want to live together."

Em thought about that. "Last week when I was there, we saw them kissing."

Aimi shrugged. "I think it's more about America. Mom loves Japan so much, and Dad says he can't live there. And if one of them has to be unhappy, it'll have to be Mom because he's the one making a living."

Em's eyes were big. "Wow!"

Aimi looked down, her thick black hair falling forward to hide her face.

"Wow!" Em repeated. "And what about you? Will you live in America or Japan?"

"I have to choose." Aimi's voice was small.

"Wow!" Em whispered. "Wow!"

"I don't know what to do." It was a pitiful wail.

"Well—" Em started, but then stopped. What could she say that would help?

For long minutes they were silent. Then Aimi picked up the Ken and Barbie dolls. She hefted them, as if she was balancing them against each other. "I think girls are supposed to be with their moms."

Em couldn't nod or shake her head. She could only watch her best friend struggle to decide something so horrible.

Finally, Aimi made Barbie kick Ken. "Stupid old Skerry," she said.

In the next three months, Em barely saw Aimi except at school. And then, Aimi and her mom moved back to Japan. They did a video chat now and then, but each time, Aimi was more Japanese than American. Her clothes changed and her English came with a hint of an accent. She had chosen to be Japanese and her choice came true.

Dr. Bari wanted her to make a choice, too. He was so passionate about the Phoke. She supposed a race in danger of going extinct would need someone like him in order for his people to survive. But the cost to individual lives was massive. Bobbie Fleming had felt forced to give up her daughter for adoption; afterwards, Ms. Fleming refused to marry another Phoke, just for the sake of genetics. So she had no husband and no children, only a career and a difficult brother.

Perhaps every adopted kid wonders: what would her biological mother's life have been like if she hadn't gotten pregnant? Was Em doomed to repeat her mother's problems just because of genetics? Or did she have real choices? Because of her genetics, she could out swim most humans. What else was determined by her particular genetics?

Em finally had her sandwich made. She sat opposite of Dr. Bari, took a bite, and mumbled through a full mouth, "Did you know my father?"

"I met Darien." The words were clipped. Now he was the angry one.

"You didn't like him," she said flatly.

"Didn't like what he did to your mother. She was so clear-headed, so determined, until she met Darien again in college."

Em couldn't hold back the words: "But it was her choice, her life."

Dr. Bari took a drink and swallowed. He didn't meet her gaze, just looked up at the ceiling. His voice was rough with emotion. "Did you know that Bobbie and I are twins? Growing up, we were always together. On everything. And she promised me, promised her twin, that she'd only marry someone who was Mer."

"Did you marry a Mer?"

Dr. Bari nodded. "Laxmi lives in New Jack, our city in the Pacific Ocean just off Seattle. I work in Seattle but spend most weekends in New Jack."

"Was it an arranged marriage?"

"No. I was sent to Jubal-Khan in hopes that I'd meet someone. And we were both lucky. Laxmi is a Phoke doctor, so we went through medical school together."

"And you wanted Bobbie to marry a Phoke, too?"

Dr. Bari looked away. When he spoke, his voice was harsh. "With Darien, she betrayed me."

"She betrayed you?" Em was outraged. "You betrayed her. You no longer cared if she was happy."

"There were deeper issues!"

"And you don't like me because I represent her betrayal?"

"In some ways, you remind me so much of your mom," he said slowly. "Oh, your dark hair and something in the way you move—that's Darien. You slouch, and confidence oozes out of you. He did that same thing."

Em thought of how Jake slouched into the coffee shop that day in August. His moves, his face—she was immediately attracted. But he'd been difficult to talk with until she'd spilled a cup of coffee in the lap of some ELLIS officer, and Jake defended her. She'd let him walk her home after that. And every time he tried to talk or do something funny to get her attention, he pulled her in as surely as an expert fisherman cranking in a big fish. Jake had her hook, line and sinker.

She couldn't jump off his hook; she didn't want to jump off his hook. Shelby Bulmer, for example, could never be her boyfriend just because he was also a quarter Phoke. She doubted someone a quarter Japanese would claim her affections, either. Her affections were already taken. Love had nothing to do with family or genetics. Even Romeo and Juliet knew that.

Em thought the conversation was over, but Dr. Bari pushed back against her decision. "Will you reconsider? Will you come to Aberforth Hills for high school?"

Em remembered a long-ago conversation with her adopted sister. Marisa had been ten or eleven and Em was only five or six. Because she was so much older, it was one of the last times that Marisa played dolls with Em. From somewhere, Mom had ordered an Asian baby doll for Em while Marisa had a large American Girl doll. They named them Chika and Arabella. They sat on the deck—it must have been summer because it was warm. Marisa brought out her china tea set, and they had milk and graham crackers.

Marisa fed Arabella and then leaned over to Chika. "Who was your birth mother?" she asked.

Em screwed up her face. "Her momma birthed her."

Marisa nodded. "Yes. But now, you're her momma. You didn't birth her. You're the adopted mother."

"Oh," Em said. The family talked about birth mothers and adopted mothers; nothing was kept secret from either girl. They knew they didn't have the same birth mothers or fathers, and that's why they looked so different.

Marisa tapped Chika's forehead and repeated, "Who was your birth mother?"

Irritated, Em pulled Chika back into a hug. "Who cares?"

Taken aback, Marisa tilted her head and stared at Em. "Well. Maybe I care."

"Why?" To Em, it was obvious that birth mothers didn't matter. They were gone.

Marisa tossed her head. "Well, you're too little to understand," she said with the superiority of an almost teenager. "Sometimes, you know, I just wonder if I'll ever get to meet my mom and dad."

Em smiled ruefully at the memory. She had been too young to understand. Now, at fifteen, it did matter. Finding out that her mother was a member of a hidden race of Phoke, well, it did matter. She just didn't know how it mattered or how much it mattered. The only thing she knew for sure was that she loved Mom and Dad, the only family she'd known growing up. She'd hate anyone who made her try to choose.

"No," she said firmly. "I want to go home to Bainbridge Island. And I want to talk with my parents. Today."

"I'm sorry, but you can't do that yet."

"Why not?" she demanded.

"Because you're not well enough to leave. I told them you'd be in isolation for about a month, so they are confident you are doing well. But I can't allow you to tell them all about Aberforth Hills." He paused, then smiled wryly. "Wait until the day after Christmas. You can talk to them then."

"Why then?"

"Contingency Plan."

"What's that?" Em asked.

"You'll find out." He stood. "You're welcome here in your family's home for as long as you stay in Aberforth Hills. Make yourself comfortable." Before she could speak, he held up a hand. "I'll stay out of your way. You may come and go as you like. Just take it easy so you don't relapse."

Dr. Bari pushed back his chair, stood, and strode away, leaving Em to stare at the sandwich on her plate and wonder, "What is the Contingency Plan?"

SUBMARINE WRECK

December 23

"Chlorine gas?" Jake asked. "That's what sank the sub?"

Mom nodded. "When the sea water hit the chemical batteries, it released chlorine gas that filled the submarine. "If they didn't come up for air, all of the Nazi crew would have died."

"Once it surfaced, the British Navy captured them. Right?"

Mom leaned on the deck railings and stared ahead. They were twelve miles out to sea just off Aberdeenshire, north of Edinburgh. The waters were choppy, but nothing the Royal Navy couldn't handle. "The sub's crew didn't even put up much of a fight."

"So, how did the sea water get into the sub and the battery compartment?"

Mom turned to him, her eyes twinkling with mirth. After a good night's sleep, they both looked better. Jake's temperature was back to a normal 108, and his stomach wound wasn't an angry red now, just a dull red. His faster and hotter Risonian physiology meant a rapid recuperation, and it was good to know that Earth's antibiotics worked on Risonians.

"You're going to like this," Mom said. "When a submarine goes underwater, it's under a lot of pressure. One of the biggest engineering problems was the toilet."

"No way," Jake interrupted.

Laughing, Mom said, "Yes. The toilets were complicated. To flush something away, you opened a series of valves in a specific order. Someone got it wrong and the toilet backed up, letting seawater flood the sub. When it reached the battery compartment under the toilet, the acids in the battery reacted with the sea water and gave off chlorine gas. That meant they had to come up for fresh air. When the British arrived, the German commander scuttled his boat rather than let it be captured."

"And they know where this happened?"

"Yes, in Cruden Bay. And we're going down to see the German submarine U-1206."

"What depth?"

"70 meters," she said.

Jake shrugged. That was deep for Risonian anatomy, but easily within their ability.

The boat shuddered to a stop, the morning sun glinting off the gentle swells. Jake and Mom turned to the group of military officers who waited for them.

"Ma'am, it will take us a few minutes to put on our scuba gear," said Captain Heath Bulmer. "Do you need anything?"

The tall British Navy diver had met them at their hotel and driven them to the dock where they climbed on board a large Navy boat. On board, he'd introduced the other divers. A lean Hispanic woman, Captain Meryl Puentes, represented the U.S. Navy, while the Greek Navy was represented by a swarthy man with a huge mustache and eyebrows, Colonel Sammy Vanzetti. Other uniformed men were from Estonia, China, Argentina, and Japan. They were handpicked to represent the United Nations team currently working with the Risonian Ambassador.

The team quickly adjusted equipment, settling heavy bottles of air on their backs, adjusting gloves and checking their breathing apparatuses. Everyone was a pro. They expected to dive for less than 30 minutes, all that humans could endure at the 70-80 meter depth.

Mom had cautioned Jake, saying, "They won't have long to look around. Stay with the group, and when they want to go up, we go up. Match their speed. Don't do anything to make them worry."

Jake rolled his eyes and nodded. He knew how to hide his real capabilities. That was his entire life, hiding in plain sight.

They waited until Captains Bulmer and Puentes had entered the water and then dove in. The others wore full scuba gear to protect them from the cold, but Mom had a simple one-piece swimming suit while Jake wore a pair of swim shorts and a wetsuit vest. The vest kept his stomach wound protected, and hidden, but it still left his armpits and gills free. The Navy officers would want to see their gills and Velcroed legs in action. Like all the divers, the Risonians wore a belt from which hung a slate and special marking pen to write on for communication. Within moments, everyone was in the water. The Earthlings carried high-intensity lights, and someone—

behind the scuba gear, Jake thought it was the Argentinian—carried an underwater camera.

Mom wouldn't like that, Jake thought, but he understood the Earthling's unease around them.

Jake zipped his legs together and undulated his body, heading downward. Captain Bulmer's face mask was outlined in a fluorescent yellow, which made him easy to pick out of the crowd. Jake was careful to stay behind Bulmer, letting him lead.

Mom swam easily. In fact, Jake couldn't remember the last time she'd been in the water for a swim. Maybe it was last August when they were with Dad at Gulf Shores, Alabama. She'd enjoyed the Gulf of Mexico with its warm waters and sugar-like sand. Here, in the colder waters, she swam with an energy and grace, circling up and around and back down to keep track of all the divers.

They'd only have fifteen minutes at the submarine's depth, and then they'd have to go back up slowly to prevent DCS, or decompression sickness.

The submarine lay half buried in the sand. In the glare of the Navy lights, it seemed pewter gray, though Jake thought it was originally painted blue. The sub looked like a strange hotel for marine life, what with its barnacles, darting fish, floating jellyfish and—Jake stopped, suddenly suspicious.

One rock was too still. The surrounding rocks had growths that waved back and forth gently in the water currents, but this one waved just a tad out of sync. Jake suspected the rock was an octopus. He swam down until he was a foot away from the rock. Maybe it was just a rock. It certainly looked like one. Captain Puentes had followed him, and she pointed a camera at him.

Jake gave her a thumbs up, and then poked at the rock.

The octopus flinched and squirted away.

Jake flinched, too, his heart thumping at the octopus's sudden transformation. Then, with an inward grin, he chased the octopus down the length of the submarine until it suddenly did its disappearing act and became a rock again.

Looking around, only Puentes had followed him. The others were gesturing to them to come back, pointing upward.

The time had flown by. Jake's water breathing was so easy and natural that he'd almost forgotten that the Earthlings relied on the scuba gear. Mom had explained what "scuba" meant: Self-Contained Underwater Breathing Apparatus. Mostly, it meant they had to be vigilant about how much time they spent underwater.

As he turned and swam back toward the group, he glanced back at Puentes. Around her mouth regulator, she managed to frown. Above her face mask, her eyebrows were squeezed together. She was angry.

Jake guessed it was because she'd lost track of time, too. He shrugged it off. They'd be up top soon, and she'd forget it.

Now, it was a matter of timing their ascent. Watching their depth gauges and watches carefully, they rose a certain distance and waited at that depth a prescribed amount of time for their bodies to adjust to the different pressures.

Jake chaffed at the hurry-up-and-wait progression to the surface. He kicked around above and below the waiting divers, trying to entertain himself. Puentes stayed with him, going up and down with him. He motioned her to join the others who were stationary, but she shook her head and continued the Follow-the-Leader game, as if Jake might suddenly dart off if she wasn't on his tail.

On the third level, a school of herring descended on them. It was a glittering mass of motion, as fish circled, darted, and swam in unfathomable formations. The divers kept their depth consistent, but with difficulty. In the glistening silver, Jake lost sight of Puentes. Finally, he thought, his shadow was gone.

But then, below them and sinking deeper, he spied Puentes, who was grabbing at her leg.

She had a cramp, he realized. Fear grabbed at his stomach. This was a serious problem for a human!

He darted through the silver mass of fish, shoving them away with his hands and arms to reach his mother. He pointed downward.

Together, they thrust their leg-tails to go deeper and catch up to Puentes. When she saw them coming, Jake realized that Puentes was in a panic. She tried to evade them, kicking hard, but then pulling up because of the cramp.

Mom grabbed Puentes's arm, but the diver wriggled around, trying to escape. Jake grabbed her other arm, and together they forced Puentes to stop. Struggling to hold on and get his slate around, Jake managed to write, "DCS! Let us help you!"

Vehemently, Puentes shook her head.

Jake realized that her thinking was impaired. If they didn't get help, she would freak out and not make it. He flapped his hands at his mom and used the miniature waves of water to tell her that he was going for help.

Mom nodded. Hurry, she seemed to say.

Above them, the other divers were still ascending. Jake quickly darted upward, using his leg-tail to powerfully speed through the water. He saw Bulmer's yellow-trimmed mask and turned to intercept him.

Bulmer started backing away as if Jake was attacking.

But Jake stopped ten feet away and held up his slate for Bulmer to read.

The diver dropped the harpoon, which was attached to his arm with a long rope. Instead, he grabbed his own slate. "Puentes has DCS?"

Jake nodded, then lifted his arms and shrugged as if to ask, "What do I do?"

The diver pointed to his regulator and wrote, "No air. Can't go back down."

Jake pointed upward and quickly wrote, "Going up for help."

It was a tense half-hour. Jake quickly explained to the ship's captain what was happening. They called for a helicopter and a compression chamber.

Then Jake carried down a couple more scuba tanks. Bulmer took a fresh tank and accompanied Jake back to where Mom was holding Puentes. At the sight of Bulmer, Puentes seemed to calm a bit and let him hold her instead of Mom. One tactic to deal with DCS was to dive deeper and hope that the gas bubbles recompressed and took some stress off the diver's body.

Slowly, they began surfacing again, following protocols.

An hour later, they broke the surface with Puentes, and the waiting medical personnel took over.

Slumped over on the medical cot, breathing a special mixture of air, Puentes waved at Jake. She pulled aside her mask and said with slurred speech. "You did that deliberately. You went for the octopus to pull me deeper and keep me there longer."

Jake was speechless. "No! I wouldn't do that!"

The other divers turned to stare at Jake.

"She's not thinking clearly," he protested. "I looked at the octopus, but I didn't do it to keep her under."

Captain Bulmer, holding his yellow-rimmed mask, looked grimly from Puentes to Jake.

Jake had always felt like he owed the universe for not dying when he was ten. Volcanologists had invited his step-dad Swann to take a look at the crater of the Ja-Ram Volcano on the western edge of Tizzalura. Swann had brought Jake, saying it was a good field trip for him.

Standing on the edge of the crater, he balanced on a small ledge of hardened volcanic rock. Looking at the molten lava bubbling below, Jake's face felt scorched. He shifted his feet, thinking that he'd back away. Instead, his boots knocked the ledge somehow, and the brittle rock broke off. He slipped, falling onto his back and sliding on the rock like it was a polished glass slide. He flailed, hands reaching for something, anything. At the last second, Swann caught his wrist. Another scientists caught Swann around the waist. Still, the momentum swept them forward until Jake dangled by his arm over the crater.

Oh, maybe if he'd fallen, the edges of the crater's bowl were hard enough to hold his weight. Maybe he would have been able to climb back up. Maybe. . .

All he knew was that he should've died. He vowed to help anyone else he ever saw who was in trouble. The fact that they now questioned his actions and motives crushed him. He would never deliberately do the equivalent of hanging someone over a volcano's crater. Never.

Jake lifted his hands in an appeal for understanding.

Bulmer pursed his lips and turned away to take off his gear.

The Army nurses gave Puentes a shot that knocked her out, and lifted her into a portable compression chamber for a medflight back to the Edinburgh hospital where there waited a specialist in decompression problems.

Mom reached over and touched Bulmer's shoulder. "Puentes," she said. "Is she related to General Puentes of the ELLIS Forces?"

"His only daughter, only child."

Mom and Jake groaned together. General Puentes would never believe this was an accident caused by Puentes being too compulsive about staying close to Jake.

Captain Heath Bulmer said, "I don't know if you tried to keep her under too long or not. But if you weren't there, she would've died. I'll make sure that's in my report." He unzipped his wetsuit and shrugged it off his shoulders. Underneath, he wore a tight wicking t-shirt.

"Thank you," Mom said formally. "We'd appreciate your independent and unbiased report."

Jake was relieved, but still worried. General Puentes didn't strike him as the most reasonable person. He doubted that the General would believe the event was innocent on Jake's part.

Captain Bulmer pulled off his scuba boots, and then straightened. "I'm all done in for today. But tomorrow, on Christmas Eve, are you available for brunch? I'd like to take the two of you for a real Scottish Christmas brunch. We'll have Scottish oatmeal, scones and tea. And a few special things for Christmas."

Mom studied him with a politician's eye. "That sounds lovely. But I have to ask, will it just be a Scottish brunch, or are you wanting to discuss other things?"

"We know that Jake saved Seattle from a Mt. Rainier explosion. And now, he's saved a diver whose father has attacked you personally. He's acted with bravery and generosity. We believe that Rison's cause should get a wider hearing. We believe that discussions are always interesting."

Jake wanted to laugh. Bulmer's manner was noncommittal, and his phrasing was intentionally vague and vaguely complimentary; he was a good politician.

Mom's eyes lit up at the politic-speak. "Very well. Christmas Eve Brunch."

KIDNAPPED

December 24

The next morning, a little before 9 a.m., Jake walked through the adjoining doorway into his mother's room and interrupted a lively conversation. He was yawning, but he was finally getting used to the time zone change from Seattle. His stomach was already growling. He'd already packed his waterproof backpack with headphones and music. He was ready in case the discussion turned boring.

David sat on the edge of a hard chair drinking from a tiny espresso cup, while Colonel Barbena and Colonel Lett paced in front of the large windows overlooking Edinburgh. His mother sat calmly at a small desk clicking on something on her computer screen.

David was saying, "Jillian wants to see the changing of the guard and do all the touristy things in London."

Colonel Barbena scowled. "You can't be serious. It might seem like an innocent brunch, but—"

Arms crossed in anger, Colonel Lett put in, "—it could be a trap."

Mother waved to Jake to come in and said, "They are trying to decide what to do today while we are guests of Captain Bulmer."

Captain Barbena turned to him, "We need to go London to check security for the Ambassador to move there tomorrow."

"Which is why," Mom said, "you should both run down to London this morning. Come back late tonight or early tomorrow. Captain Bulmer is a good man. He helped us with the diver who was in trouble, and he's the sort that seems trustworthy."

"Seems," Colonel Lett said scornfully.

"Jillian and I want to go to London for the day, too," David added. He motioned for Jake to try some of the espresso. "We'll do the tourist thing in London so Jillian can get pics for social media. What would we do here but wait around till you're not busy?"

"You should let them go, Mom," Jake said. He stretched his arms high, which made him realize that his stomach wound was even better today. Barely a twinge. He poured espresso and took a piece of dry toast. "We'll be fine by ourselves for twelve hours. Right?"

Mom shut her computer's lid and nodded. "Fine. You four go to London. Jake and I will be here when you get back. And David?"

"Yes, ma'am?"

"Make sure Jillian doesn't post anything questionable. I'll trust your discretion," Mom said.

That brought a series of laughs from everyone. Jillian was so unpredictable. Mostly her photos evoked a sense of drama, but sometimes she ran off into melodrama. It would be like her to try to stage a set of photos in London about the Phantom of the Opera. Or maybe Jack the Ripper.

There came a rapid knock on the room's door. The guards and David quietly left by exiting into the adjoining room. They were all drilled in discretion and knew that they needed to be unseen. Jake gulped his espresso and crammed the toast in his mouth before he opened the door.

Bulmer—out of uniform, dressed in jeans and corduroy jacket—nodded pleasantly and asked, "Are you ready for a great Scottish brunch? Are you hungry?"

"Mmm," mumbled Jake through his mouthful of toast.

"Ready," Mom said.

Jake grabbed his backpack. They pulled on jackets and followed the captain downstairs, and through the hotel lobby to a waiting white van. Bulmer opened the passenger door for Mom and ushered her inside. Two men with military haircuts already sat in back. Jake hesitated, uncertain, at the door. The men looked like soldiers and the driver looked military, too. Were they wrong to trust Captain Bulmer?

Bulmer waved at the two in back and said, "My friends, Syd and Les." He nodded toward the driver. "That's Edmund Frisk, the driver and our esteemed cook for the day."

Mom was already buckling her seat belt, so Jake reluctantly climbed in. As the van pulled into the heavy traffic around their hotel, Jake asked, "Where are we going for brunch? You didn't say."

Bulmer didn't answer, instead waving at a taxi that cut in front of them. Edmund, the driver, broke into a rapid curse, talking rapidly in a deep Scottish accent that Jake barely understood.

Mom and Jake looked at each other and shrugged. They'd find out soon enough. The toast hadn't been nearly enough, though, and Jake's stomach was rumbling.

Watching the road told Jake almost nothing since he knew so little of Edinburgh. He was surprised when they pulled up at a marina and stopped.

Bulmer opened the door and bowed, "This way, Ambassador."

Jake and Mom climbed out.

"Where are we going, Captain?" Mom looked up at him disapprovingly.

"Sailing! Of course. I'm a Navy man and I've got this private sailing boat, *Ruby*. Edmund Frisk is a great cook and he'll be serving us."

Mom stopped short and put her hands on her hips in a gesture of defiance. "Am I being a fool to go with you?" she asked bluntly.

Jake gave her credit: she surprised the Captain.

"You are quite perceptive, Ambassador. This isn't quite what it seems. But you can trust me that this is something you want to do. More than that, I cannot say."

Mom prided herself on being a good judge of character, so Jake waited. She looked Captain Bulmer up and down. To his credit, he didn't flinch away from her gaze.

Jake almost wanted to laugh at the image of his tiny mother defiantly weighing the characters of these burly men.

She turned to the three men—their escorts, or their guards, depending on your viewpoint. She gazed at them, as well, and no one turned aside.

"Will we be back by 4p.m. to meet with my staff?" she asked.

Bulmer cleared his throat. "Not likely."

"This is important?" she asked, then answered her own question. "Of course, it's important if you're kidnapping us."

Jake gulped at her words, but held steady beside her, not allowing himself to flinch or naysay her comments in any way.

Bulmer merely nodded, his eyes lighting with a newfound respect.

"Very well," she said to Bulmer. "We will accompany you." She turned to other men. "And Mister Frisk?"

He stepped forward. "Yes, ma'am?""

"We expect an excellent Christmas brunch. I take my tea with cream and sugar, please. And my son is famished. As usual."

Leaving the men gaping, she turned and strode to the boat. With her head high, she allowed Bulmer to give her a hand as she stepped onto *Ruby*. The wind gusted suddenly and her curls blew in her face. With misgivings, Jake followed her. The last time they boarded a vessel together, it was Puentes's yacht, and that hadn't gone well. He was grateful for the knife on his back and for the one strapped to his leg.

ABERFORTH HILLS

December 24

Ruby skimmed over the waves, her sails singing. A north wind blew cold, but Mom and Jake were sheltered behind a screen, with blankets available as they wished.

Edmund Frisk proved to be more than a capable cook in the tiny galley. He brought up a tray of steaming tea with cream, sugar, and scones, followed by bowls of Scottish oatmeal with brown sugar and raisins as toppings. Jake ate three bowls and only stopped because he didn't want to appear rude. Mom seemed to be perfectly at ease, but as the morning wore on, Jake worried. *Ruby* was heading far out to sea.

He went to the head—the bathroom of the boat—where he had some small measure of privacy, and pulled out his cell phone to check the GPS app. As he suspected, they were heading in the direction of Aberforth Hills, the underwater city they had seen before. Good. Maybe he'd get some answers.

Finally, about noon, *Ruby* slowed, and Captain Bulmer dropped sails.

"Where are we?" Mom asked. "Will someone join us here?"

"We're going swimming," Bulmer answered. "We'll need to put on our scuba gear. Do you want a wet suit or not?"

Mom rolled her eyes. "It would've been nice to know that I'd be swimming. I would have worn a swim suit."

She had just had custom-made a long-sleeved swimsuit with the arm-pits cut out so her gills would have access to the water. She'd been anxious to try it.

"We took the liberty of buying you a new suit," Bulmer said apologetically. He held up a black suit identical to the one she had bought.

So, Jake thought, they've been following every move we make. He took an uncertain breath. Who were these people? Why had they monitored them so closely? None of this sounded good.

Bulmer also handed Jake a bundle with a swim suit and wet suit vest. Taking it, Jake's hands shook with worry.

The captain stepped aside to allow the Risonians to go below deck to change clothes.

Downstairs, Jake whispered, "We're at Aberforth Hills, the underwater city. We'll get to see it."

Mom nodded soberly, "We'll meet whoever lives there. And I think we're in for a surprise."

A few minutes later, they joined Bulmer and his men. They would leave only Edmund Frisk to man the sailboat.

They dove. Cold hit Jake for a few moments until his magma-sapiens blood took over and the temperature seemed normal. Bulmer and his troops all wore headlights, but the streams of light barely penetrated ten feet ahead. He kept Mom in sight, lest there was another trap planned. But Bulmer and his crew just kicked deeper and deeper until—

The light from Aberforth Hills started in a slow, gentle, distant glow. Soon, however, Bulmer and his crew turned off their headlights and swam directly for the light. Jake watched Mom and tried to see it from her point of view. She'd been raised in an underwater city on Rison, and when she took Jake for visits with his grandparents, he'd been able to explore some. The anatomical differences between Risonians and these Phoke, or whatever they called themselves, was obvious in the architecture and the city.

Risonian buildings had windows and doors that were open to the sea, like cottages on the windblown Scottish shore might open their windows to let in a sea breeze. The buildings in front of them now were a mass of walls, with few windows except on the newest-looking buildings. Risonians truly lived in the sea, with the currents sweeping through city streets to cleanse them of debris. Homes could be shuttered against storms, but usually they were filled with water and open to the currents.

This was a Mer city, or a Phoke city, if you liked the modern term. From the gossip he'd picked up, the Phoke had to breathe air every 30 minutes or so. They needed airtight buildings and pumps to bring air down, or air convertors of some kind.

The oldest buildings—those covered in barnacles and crabs—were shaped like a bell. Often there was a red arrow pointing down, which Jake guessed was a universal symbol pinpointing a moon pool entrance, such as they had on the Seastead in Puget Sound. The newest buildings were connected by a series of tubes, apparently pumped full of air—probably an expensive and difficult matter. Inside the tunnels, figures scurried back and forth.

The city was immense. Jake was hard pressed to even guess its population.

Bulmer motioned them toward a hill and they swam upward to reach the bottom floor of a massive structure that seemed like it was four or five stories tall. This was one of the seven fabled hills of Aberforth Hills, and atop it was an important building. A large tunnel led into the building. Bulmer swam under the tunnel following a red arrow, and a moment later, they saw his form emerge inside the tunnel.

Jake and Mom raised eyebrows at each other, but they followed Bulmer to enter the moon pool. Near the tunnel's entrance was a stack of chamois cloths that they used to dry off, and then placed the wet towels in a basket. Presumably, they would be laundered and returned here at some point. Bulmer pulled off a waterproof backpack and pulled out t-shirts for each of the men and a longer t-shirt dress for mom. They donned them over their swim suits or wet suits. Apparently, it was okay to appear in such garb in polite Phoke society. Finally, he handed around flip-flops, the correct size, of course.

Nearby, a golf cart zipped by. Jake had no idea how it hovered about half a foot above the ground, or how it built up such speed. Obviously, the Phoke had advanced science and engineering skills.

"Where are we?" Mom asked Captain Bulmer.

Her voice was funny, high pitched. Jake realized that the tunnels were full of Tri-Mix gas, not just surface air. Because it included helium as one of the three gases, everyone would sound like a cartoon character.

"Ambassador Quad-de, may I be the first to welcome you to Aberforth Hills. We are taking you to meet the ruling council of the Phoke and to attend their first ever press conference."

The funny voice almost made it sound like a comedy routine. But Jake was sure that this was deadly serious.

FLASH MOB

December 24
London on Christmas Eve had been, as they say, brilliant. For Jillian, David and the Risonian officers, Christmas decorations gave the dreary day a cheerfulness it lacked on any other winter day. Jillian was happy when they dropped her at a shopping center with Colonel Barbena in tow, while David and Colonel Lett did an architecture tour. The shops were cheerful and rang with Christmas songs in that wonderful British accent. Jillian bought small gifts for everyone.

When they all met up again, the bodyguards left David and Jillian at the Tower Museum while the Colonels went to the Ambassador's hotel and planned security for their stay.

Finally, they all went to Buckingham Palace to watch the "pomp and circumstance" of the changing of the guard.

Wind blew briskly, making Jillian pull up her hood. Buckingham Palace was stately in the background. She was disappointed that no one was allowed inside the massive black-iron gate with its imposing gold crest. Rows of soldiers stood at attention wearing red jackets, black pants and the crazy-big fuzzy-hats.

Jillian punched David. "Wish I could see you in one of those!"

He just laughed.

It was a good day, she thought. They'd been more relaxed without Jake and the Ambassador along. London was amazing, and she was already planning how to talk her mother into vacationing here next summer.

Most soldiers carried band instruments, with the trombones on the front row where their long slides wouldn't hit the person in front of them. The guards' wind-chapped cheeks were almost as red as their uniforms.

As usual, a crowd gathered to watch the changing of the guards. Jillian snapped photos with her smart phone, pausing only to upload to one or another of her social media channels. The crowd was kept off the road behind a fence. Crowd control guards wore black vests over heavy jackets, but even with all that on, they looked cold.

The band marched until it exited the palace gates. The drum major signaled, and the band lifted instruments to play its first song, a lively march. The step was odd. After each step, the soldier held his foot above the ground in a sort of stutter step, stretching out the march steps.

Suddenly, something rolled from the crowd toward the soldiers.

Jillian had to stand on tiptoe to see it: a blue ball.

One trombonist almost tripped avoiding the ball and had to run a step to catch up with the front line.

Another blue ball spun past a guard into the band's path.

These two started a trickle of blue balls spinning from somewhere in the crowd toward the marching soldier.

Jillian raised her camera phone and started videotaping.

A dozen blue balls bounced toward the marching guardsmen. And another dozen.

It was impossible to see who was rolling the balls onto the street. No one. Everyone.

She scanned her phone to photograph the crowd. An old white-haired man pulled a ball from a deep coat pocket. A small woman in a nurse's scrubs reached inside her purse for a ball. Balls bounced, rolled and clanged against each other and around the guardsmen's feet.

The band stalled, and the drum major marched on alone, oblivious to the destruction of the carefully planned march.

Jillian's face lit up with understanding. "A flash mob!"

The ground around the guardsmen's feet was dangerously cluttered with balls. A saxophonist kicked at the balls trying to clear a spot, but only kicked the balls into his friends. No one could move without tripping.

Then a man stepped forward. Quickly, Jillian turned her phone camera toward him. He was nondescript. An average height man with average brown hair and average clothing—jeans and a black jacket.

In a clear voice, he called, "Blue balls because Earth is a blue planet. Earth is for Earthlings, not for Risonians."

The crowd took up the chant, "Earth is for Earthlings."

Jillian's breath caught in a sharp pain: these people were protesting against Rison. She knew it happened, but had never seen it, never been in such a situation.

By now the Drum Major realized what had happened, and the black-vested guards looked at each other, trying to decide what to do.

The chant lasted less than a minute, before people turned and walked away.

The guards could do nothing but watch them leave. They hadn't actually thrown balls at the guard. They hadn't hurt anyone. If you asked one person about it, they'd just say their ball accidentally fell onto the street.

Mostly, people left with a smile. The flash mob had won the day.

David pulled Jillian away, too. They walked briskly back to the car with their bodyguards on high alert.

"Why?" Jillian asked. Even to herself, her voice sounded forlorn. *Earth is for Earthlings*, the chant still echoed in her head. Risonians were going to die by the millions and Earthlings didn't care.

"Should I post the video?" she asked David. She always posted on social media. Always. To even question that—the flash mob had shocked her to her core.

Bitterly, David nodded. There were bound to be lots of clips on the news and on social media, he explained. She might as well be the one with the scoop. It kept their cover intact.

There were so few Risonians on Earth right now. It was ironic, Jillian thought, that they'd been there to see the protest.

The anti-Risonian sentiment chafed at her the rest of the day as they drove back to Edinburgh. By the time they were back in Edinburgh late on Christmas Eve, everyone was exhausted.

When they tried to check in with the Ambassador, though, they found that she and Jake were missing. Her cell phone was turned off, not even ringing. And there was a letter in the Ambassador's hand-writing telling Colonel Lett to wait 48 hours before taking action. All would be clear on Christmas morning.

Colonel Lett told David and Jillian, "Get some sleep. I'll investigate. If we've heard nothing by tomorrow morning, we'll tear this planet apart to find them."

THE CONTINGENCY PLAN

December 24

Captain Bulmer escorted Jake and Mom to a tiny room with twin beds, rather like a cramped hotel room. He refused to answer any questions. He just shook his head and said, "I'll be back in the morning."

Before they could respond, he was gone.

He had abandoned them.

A guard stationed at their door refused to let them wander about. Supper—an excellent fish stew—was brought in and they ate alone. Later, servants appeared to clear up. Jake tried to talk with them, but they refused to answer any questions.

After a boring evening, Dayexi gave in. She found pajamas in the closet—of course, they were her size—and readied for bed. As she turned out the light, she told Jake, "This has been the worst holiday ever. I hope Christmas day is better."

Jake tossed and turned. Finally, he slipped on headphones and cranked up the volume, listening to his favorite Risonian opera; it was about Killia, the mythical founder of the capital city of Tizzalura—Jake's home town on Rison. Dad had told him the story of how Rome was established by twins, Romulus and Remus, who had been raised by wolves. But this opera was better. Killia had been one of the first Risonians to leave the ocean, and he had fought wild beasts to establish a city on the high volcanic plateau. The songs were full of animals roaring, clanging battles, and a love that stretched from the highest volcanic mountains to the deepest oceans. Full of life, Risonian life. It was his music. He was a Risonian and he would listen to opera all night long if he wanted, he thought defiantly, even if he was locked up in a tiny room in the middle of a crazy, alien Phoke city.

Killia and Mawgoritza (usually called Mawg) weren't supposed to fall in love because they came from warring political families. But instead of a half-baked idea that got them both killed like crazy Shakespeare's ill-fated Romeo and Juliet, these Risonians were smarter. Instead, they walked out of the oceans and far enough inland to establish a home.

At first, they had to fight big cat-like predators to survive. Mawg stood watch with weapons drawn while Killia built them a log cabin. Then Killia stood guard while Mawg tried to figure out how to tend the food-plants they wanted and make it work. They were the first gardeners on Rison, and later, the first agriculture tycoons. Within twenty years, their *wolkevs* were sold in every market under water. And as people developed a taste for *wolkev* jam, pastries, drinks and more, Killia and Mawg claimed even more land. The extensive holdings— and love of all things *wolkev*—came from these ancestors of the Quad-des.

Jake knew this story and the opera like it was his own story. And it was so much stronger than the Mer stories of building underwater cities. Killia faced many big cat predators and killed them. One cat-hide was still a rug in Swann's room. The Mer colonized the seas, but only because they learned the right architecture, the bell jar, and then improved it as technology improved. Killia colonized the land of Tizzalura because he was strong and confident. He didn't have to rely on a particular style of architecture to colonize.

Jake wondered if he was being arrogant. He believed the Risonian struggles were harder, their triumphs deeper. Risonians were better than Earthings and Phokes. Now that was arrogant! Exactly like General Puentes, who thought Earth was the best, the strongest. No, Jake had to try to understand, and especially, to respect these other races and cultures.

At last, weary with the struggle of trying to be big-hearted—and failing—he yawned, turned off his music, and lay down to sleep.

〜〜〜　〜〜〜　〜〜〜

December 25

At 8:30 a.m., a knock at their door startled them. Jake opened the door to an unfamiliar military man.

"So sorry," said the officer. "Captain Bulmer regrets that he can't escort you himself. I'm sent to take you to the—" he paused "—the event."

Finally, Jake thought, *something is going to happen. And whatever it is, they still don't trust us to understand.*

He and Mom had decided to wear their swim suits under their clothes just in case they had to swim to the surface. The lack of trust worked both ways.

They followed the soldier as he wound through a confusing array of hallways until they came to a large room with a sign that read, "Observation Room." Inside, one wall held a podium in front of a bank of curtains. Rows of chairs were set up in a semi-circle around the podium. It wasn't a large number of chairs, perhaps 30-40. Whatever was about to happen, it was for a small audience.

Their escort indicated a couple chairs in the corner. "As a courtesy, you're allowed to observe, but do not participate or you'll be removed." His voice came out in a high-pitched squeak.

Mom's eyebrow raised, but simultaneously they both realized what this meant; this room was using the Tri-Mix air, which meant that humans were coming. The lighting highlighted the podium and left them in shadows. They'd be inconspicuous.

Jake motioned to the bigger wing-chair and said, "You take that one."

Mom had that worried expression which made her nose wrinkle.

Jake shivered. Curiosity was killing him, as the American expression went. But even deeper, an unreasonable fear struck at his gut: whatever was going to happen, it wouldn't be good for Rison.

To stop the worry, he counted chairs. There were their two wing-chairs and five rows of folding chairs. Ten chairs in the back row--

A door near the curtains opened and a stream of people marched in. They all wore navy shirts and khaki slacks, a mix of men and women and from a variety of ages. Looking closer, Jake saw that the navy shirts had an AH for Aberforth Hills, small and decorous, embroidered on the shirt's pocket. On the right side of the podium stood eight women and four men—

The double doors at the rear of the conference room flung open and a flood of people crowded in, chattering and looking around. Some headed for the curtains, but the Phoke staff turned them back to the chairs. Roughly half the group was dressed formally, in jacket and ties or in dresses and heels. The other half wore jeans and sweatshirts and carried large video cameras on their shoulders. New crews! Too many to count quickly.

This was a press conference. Jake recognized half a dozen of the news anchors as the bigwigs of each major station. Now that he looked, he recognized logos on the cameras. There were crews from CNN, Fox, ABC, CBS, NBC, BBC, Al-Jazeera, Euro News, Deutsche Welle, and others that he didn't know but assumed were European, African or Asian news crews. This wasn't a small local press conference. These were hand-picked international stars. This was a major press conference.

Fear struck at Jake's gut. Instinctively, he grabbed at Mom's hand.

She gripped him tightly, too. "Just watch," she murmured. "Nothing else we can do right now."

Reassured that inaction was the best action, Jake released her hand and shrank back into the shadows of his wing chair.

Jake started mentally sorting people. The news anchors were formally dressed, while the casual dress was for the cameramen. The BBC lady wore a startlingly blue cashmere sweater, black skirt and not-made-for-walking-heels. Her cameraman had a walrus mustache, dark glasses, heavy boots and thick coat. The Fox News man wore a suit, and his dark hair had greying sideburns. Conservative in dress, at his neck was a red perfectly-knotted silk tie. His voice was smooth, but oily and loud. His camerawoman was a chubby woman wearing jeans and sweatshirt, tennis shoes, and a New York Yankees baseball cap over short hair.

The light over the podium suddenly grew brighter.

A Phoke official stepped to a microphone and called, "Ladies and gentlemen. First, let me apologize for your squeaky voices."

A high-pitched titter rippled across the room.

The official continued, "You are currently 90 meters, or 270 feet, deep in the ocean. At this depth, you need a different air or your body will collect gas in your muscles and you'll get the dreaded bends, or decompression sickness. We are just making sure you stay healthy."

Fox News Suit immediately signaled his cameraman and started narrating, "We are deep under the ocean." He was probably a deep bass, but his voice was a strange soprano. "I sound like a teenager because we're breathing a strange mix of air." He paused and ran a finger across his neck, a sign to the cameraman to stop recording.

"What's this air called?" he asked in a loud squeak.

"Tri-Mix. It's a mixture of helium, nitrogen and oxygen."

With the new information, Suit started his intro again.

The announcer, though, called for attention and assigned each news crew a guide. The Phoke guides moved to stand beside their assigned crew, introduced themselves and chatted. For now, though, they refused to answer any questions.

The BBC Blue Lady demanded, "Why are we here? Why all this cloak and dagger?"

"We're waiting for the official announcement," her guide said. "After that, we're encouraged to answer all of your questions. Be patient a few more minutes."

The conference room was noisy with expectation. The reporters and camera operators were nervous, unsure of what would happen. One camerawoman searched along the wall for a plug-in. The Al-Jazeera reporter started recording an introduction, but stepped backward and stumbled on a chair. Everyone turned to stare at the clatter. One skinny cameraman stretched and yawned, then slumped into a chair, pulled his cap over his eyes and tried to sleep.

At precisely 9 a.m. Greenwich time, a man and woman marched into the room, along with several other officials at their back. No one could've looked less like Mer folk than these two professionals in their business suits. The first was Dr. Mangot, who had treated Jake at the Edinburgh Hospital. Thinking about it, Jake wasn't surprised that she was Phoke, the way she tended that aquarium in the hospital's lobby. It wasn't a menial task for her, but a labor of love. Now he saw that it was a way for her to quietly say that she was a mermaid without actually saying it.

The other person shocked Jake: it was Dr. Bari, Em's doctor from Seattle. Gripping the arms of his chair, Jake wanted to scream questions: How did you get here? You a Phoke? What did that mean for Em and her illness?

Jake vowed to corner Dr. Bari as soon as possible and find out if Em was here somewhere. A sudden hope sprung up, and he leaned forward to the edge of his seat.

Em was here!

Dr. Mangot began, "Ladies and gentlemen, as representatives of the world, we welcome you to Aberforth Hills."

Dr. Bari took over and read from a prepared statement that they were standing in the ancestral home of the Mer folk, mermaids and mermen.

The audience was silent, stunned.

Dr. Bari gave a quick rundown of the history of Aberforth Hills and concluded, "We now call ourselves the Phoke."

BBC's Blue Lady threw up her hands and swore. "What a hoax!"

"Waste of time!" the Fox News Suit agreed.

Dr. Mangot took the microphone and said, "Wait." She hesitated, and then made a decision. "I have a presentation—"

The news crews groaned in falsetto unison.

"—but I think your cameras will do more than I could. There's time for questions and explanations later. But first, let me extend an invitation. Please meet us back here at 7 p.m. tonight. We'll have cocktails, and you can ask any questions you like. We'll answer anything."

Dr. Bari and Dr. Mangot nodded to each other. "Ladies and gentlemen, we invite you to tour Aberforth Hills for yourself. You'll be restricted to only those areas where we've pumped Tri-Mix air, or your health will be in danger. Please follow your guide's lead on staying to safe areas. Otherwise, we have nothing to hide."

The two Phoke doctors stepped aside, and the curtain behind them slid sideways.

At first, there was a blur of light. Then, structures started to take shape. This was much bigger than the Seastead in Puget Sound beside Seattle. Swimming in, they'd seen the glow of light from the city. But this view from above revealed the breadth of the entire city below them, and it was much bigger than Jake had realized.

With a flourish, Dr. Bari waved at the window and said, "This is Aberforth Hills."

Sharks, or something equally large, swam past the windows, probably drawn by the light. As one, the crowd swarmed the window, jostling for the best viewing position; their guides stayed close behind, ready for questions. Other Phoke walked through the news crews handing out maps with landmarks clearly marked. In the midst of the crowd, Jake lost sight of Dr. Bari and Dr. Mangot.

BBC's Blue Lady pressed one hand on the window and stared with wide eyes. "That. Sticking up there. What is it?"

Her Phoke guide said, "That's the Gunby Clock. It sits next to the Aberforth Elementary School, and it chimes the hour, which tells the classes when to change."

"You have an elementary school?" Blue Lady squeaked incredulously.

"And a high school. I graduated from there six years ago before attending Oxford." The British accent was unmistakable, even with the squeaky voices.

The good camera operators started filming immediately. And when the on-screen personalities realized what was happening, they started talking, too, a stream of consciousness report of what they were seeing.

Their skepticism. Their awe and wonder. Their skepticism. Their awe.

Sometimes, they trailed off in wonder.

The smartest of them remembered the offer to look around the city. They took off with their Phoke guide to look around. The first tourists to Aberforth Hills. As long as they stayed in designated areas that had Tri-Mix gas, they were the first to see a new Wonder of the World.

Mom and Jake had stayed back, in the corner, until most of the news crews wandered off to explore and almost all the Phoke staff—including Dr. Bari and Dr. Mangot—had left. Only then did they walk to the window and gaze on the fabulous city.

Mom laid a hand on Jake's arm. "Tell me what you saw at the press conference." She often did this in political situations to point out the need for sharp observation.

Jake's voice trembled. "The Phoke are taking advantage of this as best they can. Putting on an amazing show."

Mom nodded, "Yes, indeed." She shook her head as if impressed by the Phoke's Contingency Plan.

"That was a brilliant press conference," Jake said. "By the end of the day, everyone on Earth will know that mermen and mermaids are real." A sadness gripped him, and he had to put his hands on the window to balance. This was awful, his worst nightmare.

Mom's whole argument for Risonian refuge on Earth was based on the fact that 70% of the planet was covered with water, and it was empty. They weren't asking Earth to share any land, just the empty oceans. The presence of the Mer crushed that argument.

It meant renegotiating everything.

It wasn't the impossibility of the task that made Jake's blood run cold. Instead, it was the time lost that was crucial. Rison's core plainly had only days left before it imploded. Not decades, not years, not months. Scientist's predictions varied widely, of course, and no one knew exactly when it would happen. Maybe they did have another year. Maybe not. They only knew it was soon. Staring out at the city, he shook his head, trying to deny that it was there. A Phoke city would ruin everything.

Time was a luxury they didn't have. The revelation of the Mer society couldn't have come at a worse time.

Jake sank to the floor, crossing his legs and leaning his forehead against the glass, fighting back nausea. Mer folk were real and had been here in Aberforth Hills for over 100 years. His mother's mission had been doomed before it started.

Doomed.

They just hadn't known it.

Above him, Mom was shaking her head, and he could see that she was running through the same barrage of emotions.

Denial: Surely this wasn't true.

Rejection of the truth: No, no, it was impossible. These weren't really Mer, but a bad dream.

Negotiation: Well, surely there was a way around the Mer, and they could still find refuge here on Earth.

Acceptance: Earth was never a real possibility for their people.

How could they move forward now?

112

Risonians were condemned to die by their own foolishness in trying to manipulate nature and by the lack of appropriate water planets for evacuation. Jake's gaze roamed over the city of Aberforth Hills, and his eyes blurred with tears. Instead of the city in front of him, he saw the underwater cities of Rison. The Quad-de family estate near Tizzalura, with their house that extended from land into the seas. There was his grandparent's house in the Holla sea, where he had spent vacations. Underwater cities were supposed to be Risonian only.

Earthlings lived on land, not in the sea.

Not in the sea.

But Mer were Earthlings, too. The truth stared back at him and struck to his depths: Risonians were doomed.

Behind them, someone said in a squeaky voice, "Excuse me."

When they turned, a Phoke staff person, a slim man in the navy and khaki uniform, said, "Dr. Mangot would like to speak with you. Do you have time now?"

OLD FRIENDS

December 25

The Phoke staff member led Mom and Jake to an elevator and pushed the button for the sixth floor, the top floor. When the elevator doors opened, he led them down a white hallway, and opened a nondescript white door and motioned for them to enter.

The room was dim with an observation window—smaller than the conference room's window, but just as arresting. Glancing around, the room was a contrast to the starkness of the rest of the building. The walls were a warm oak paneling and were hung with massive paintings of ocean scenery or ocean life. A huge carved desk sat perpendicular to the window, and behind it sat Dr. Mangot. The desk was perfectly positioned so that she could see the room and the observation window at the same time. Leather wing chairs faced the desk.

"Ah, here they are now," Dr. Mangot said. Her voice, like everyone else's, was that high pitch caused by the Tri-Mix air.

From one of the chairs, a figure rose.

"Dad?" Jake stopped still in shock.

But Mom stepped forward, a hand held out, and said in a broken voice, "You're here?"

"I came with the news crews, disguised as a cameraman," Dad said matter-of-factly.

"How'd you know to come?" she demanded.

Dad smiled wryly and reached out to hug Mom. "I didn't want you to spend Christmas without me."

She looked up angrily and tapped his chest with her forefinger. "The truth?"

"The Navy got wind of a secret press conference," he said. "We decided to crash it. Good thing, too, because we don't like surprises." He glanced back at Dr. Mangot, and his expression went grim.

Jake stepped forward. "Dad. There's so much we have to tell you!"

Dr. Mangot stood and came around from behind her desk. To Dad, she said, "I'll step out if you like. You'll want a private moment with your son."

"My adopted son," Dad said automatically.

"Your son, Blake. You don't have to pretend with me; I've done the blood work."

Dad and Mom stared at her in horror. The only real secret they still had left was the fact that Dad was Jake's real biological father. It was fine for the press to know that Dayexi's son was here on Earth, especially when they all knew that Swann Quad-de, the prime minister of the largest country on Rison, was his father. But if they knew it was possible for Risonians and humans to pro-create together, there'd be chaos. It would seal the death warrant for Rison. Earth wouldn't allow any aliens on the planet if they thought Risonians and Earthlings could intermarry and have kids. Even though Jake was created in a test tube, the knowledge of his lineage would evoke a new panic about letting the Risonians come to Earth. If the presence of the Mer had sealed their fate, Dr. Mangot could scuttle even the slimmest hopes left by releasing this information.

Dad pulled Mom and Jake behind him and stepped forward to face his old college and medical school chum. Coldly, he asked, "Bea, what do you think you know?"

"Test tube, right? It wasn't. . ." For a moment Dr. Mangot's forced smile wavered, as if she wasn't sure of the facts.

Grimly, Dad repeated, "Test tube."

Dr. Mangot gave a sigh of relief. "Anything else was unthinkable!"

"What do you want?" Dad's normally olive skin was blanched pale with anger.

A dull anger burned in Jake's mind, too. As always, he was just a pawn in a bigger game.

"Don't get so huffy and protective," Dr. Mangot said casually. "I don't want much."

"What?" Dad's fists were tight, and he jammed them into his jacket pocket.

Dr. Mangot took her time walking back around her desk. Her dark hair was pulled back into a severe pony tail that swung lightly. She pulled out the leather chair and sat. Leaning forward, arms on the desk, she waved at the leather chairs. "Please. Sit."

Numbly, Mom and Dad sank into the leather. Rigid with anger, Jake stood behind Dad's chair.

Dr. Mangot steepled her fingers and tilted her head. Her thick pony tail swung the opposite direction, giving her a balanced look. Her voice was calm, reasonable. "We have a mutual problem, and I just want to be sure we are on the same page for a solution."

Restless, Dad readjusted, inching forward to sit on the edge of the chair.

Dr. Mangot continued, "Because of the illegal invasion of our waters by the Risonians—"

Mom started to protest, but Dr. Mangot held up her hand. Even with the Tri-Mix, her voice was husky with emotion. "Let me finish. Earth's waters now contain Risonian organisms. I could say that our waters are contaminated. Or that you've brought invasive species with you deliberately. But all I'll say is this: a Risonian organism is causing Mer folk to get sick. I've isolated it in the lab, but I can't find anything that will affect it." Now her voice deepened with passion. "I need to find a cure, and I'm very practical. It's too late to go backwards and prevent it. We've got to find a cure. And for that, I want a medical expedition to Rison. Before it's too late."

Dad's jaw literally dropped. He shook his head and visibly tried to compose himself. He started to speak, stopped, and ran a hand across his face. Finally, he managed to say, "You want to go to a dying planet for medical research? Are you mad? What if it implodes while you're there?"

"It's a risk I'm willing to take." Dr. Mangot's gaze was steady, unyielding. She knew what she wanted, and she knew how to get it. Even if everyone around her disagreed.

Jake clearly understood the Phoke's changing landscape: They had new information that a Risonian organism, probably the *umjaadi*, were causing illness among the Phoke and was threatening their existence. They needed research on the organism in its natural habitat on Rison. But to get to Rison, they needed a spaceship. Which meant that they must announce to the Earth politicians for the first time that they existed.

Their old goal: Prevent the Mer from being detected.

Their new goal: Negotiate with the Earth politicians to get some Phoke doctors up to Rison to seek a cure.

Earth politicians were known for stalling; by contrast, the Phoke decision making process was lightning fast. Their survival depended upon it.

Wait. An awful thought just occurred to him. "Is that what's wrong with Em?"

"You know Emmeline Tullis?"

"Yes! Does she have an *umjaadi* infection?" Jake's voice almost broke. He'd suspected that she was a Phoke, of course. Why else would she be here in Aberforth Hills for her illness?

"Yes," said Dr. Mangot. "Her case is one of the worst. Wait. What did you call it?"

Jake was stunned. This last month, all the heartache and worry about Em, it had been because Risonians had created Seasteads on Earth! His people had given her an illness that could kill her because it was so alien to Earth. The irony struck him physically, and, weak-kneed, he sank heavily on the arm of his mother's chair. He whispered, "Is Em still sick?"

"No. For now, we've controlled the illness, and she feels good. But we don't know if she'll relapse or not."

Mom said, "That's your friend? The swimmer?"

Jake nodded. "Is she here? Can I see her?"

Dr. Mangot said, "She's here and she's fine. I'll let you see her later if she feels up to it. But for now, we need to discuss this research mission. To find the—what did you call it?"

Mom shook her head as if to wipe away confusion. "The *umjaadi*. It's an organism that lives on the *umjaadi* starfish which are often displayed in a globe, like your snow globes, I'm told. We think one was accidentally broken apart in Puget Sound, and that's where the organism escaped."

Dr. Mangot nodded. "It had to be something like that. I didn't think you'd planned it."

"No. And we had no idea it would cause any problem," Mom said. "Where would you even start such a mission?"

"Where do the *umjaadi* thrive on your planet?"

Mom shrugged. "I suppose in the south seas. That's where the starfish are."

"True," Jake said. "And that will make it even more difficult. But not impossible." The southern Bo-See Coalition was violent and would likely protest any humans visiting their homelands. But then—the planet was about to implode so what difference did it make? Would they trade spaces on an evacuation ship for a smooth access to the south seas? And he couldn't believe he was even thinking rationally about this crazy suggestion to send a research team to Rison. But if Em was sick and this was the only way to heal her—Jake would do anything to save her life. If they sent a research team to Rison, he had to be on it. He'd be able to smooth things with his step-father and with the culture. Oh, wow, the culture. Dr. Mangot had no idea of the problems such a research team would face.

Dr. Mangot leaned forward, resting her elbows on the desk. "I need to study the organism in its natural habitat and try to determine if there's anything different about the waters there. Maybe pH levels or salinity levels or something that will help us control the *umjaadi* here. Why does it live in the south seas and not in the north seas? Temperature probably isn't the limiting factor since it's in Puget Sound, so what is it? There's not enough time, no. But we've got to do something before it spreads everywhere here on Earth. Right now, it's mostly in Puget Sound, but we've already found a few traces of it in the North Pacific. But it will spread."

Dad and Mom looked at each other and Mom gave a tiny nod, a stray curl escaping to bob in front of her eyes.

Dad said, "Yes. We'll support you on this." He rapped his fist on her desk, though, and said more vehemently, "You didn't have to blackmail us to get us to agree, you know."

Dr. Mangot shrugged, her face a stone mask. "I've found that it speeds up decisions."

"You've grown cold, Bea," Dad said. "You were never this ruthless."

"With our big announcement this morning, I expect I'll need to be even more ruthless the next few years. The Phoke will need strong advocates."

"And I would've been happy to be one of those advocates," Dad said.

Dr. Mangot stood and waved toward the door. "You can still be our advocate. The United Nations will be voting within the week."

"You have enough people in places of power to pull this off within a week?" Mom was incredulous.

"Less. I want to launch on January 1. That's just six days away," Dr. Mangot said.

Mom stood and put a light hand on Dr. Mangot's arm. "I wish we could be friends."

Mangot's face tightened into a grimace. "Of course. You want our influence."

"Of course," Mom echoed. "But I also see the young idealistic woman who worked with Blake. He's always praised you and your work. I wish I'd known that woman."

Mangot's face softened and took on a far away look. "Yes. Back then, you and I could've been friends."

The door opened and a harried looking staff member scurried to hand Dr. Mangot a paper. She frowned.

"Bad news?" Dad asked.

"Weather report." She slapped the paper angrily. "They're predicting a major storm later this week. Depending on how fast it moves, we may have trouble traveling anywhere."

MOTHER AND DAUGHTER

December 25

Inside the Fleming ancestral home, the library flickered with light from a television. A high-pitched announcer said, "The Phoke city is below us."

Bobbie Fleming flipped off the TV and sat back down beside Em. The room was only lit by a couple wall sconces over a fake fireplace, leaving the bookcases in deep shadow.

The news was out. By the end of Christmas day, the whole world would know that the Mer or Phoke were real. By evening, as part of the Contingency Plan, the Phoke Bed and Breakfast website would go live, offering tourists an easy way to visit a Phoke city of choice. The accommodations would range from the warm waters of Jubal-Khan in the Indian Ocean to New Jack just outside Puget Sound. If all went as planned in the next 24 hours, the Mer B&B would be totally booked for the next year. Advertisements would flood the Internet with hundreds of images. Nothing had been left to chance in the Contingency Plan.

"What do you think of the Contingency Plan?" Bobbie asked Em.

It was a strange Christmas, Em thought wistfully. Mom, Dad, Marisa—there were no family here. Marisa was likely with her biological family anyway. She'd gone there last year and had a blast meeting relatives. It still hurt that she'd been more excited about that than joining their own family for Christmas. It was like being Em's sister didn't matter any more.

This year, everything would be dominated by the Phoke announcement. That, combined with her illness, made Christmas a bust. So, she'd make the best of it.

This was the first time she'd been alone with Bobbie since she'd talked with Dr. Bari. Em ignored the question about Phoke plans, cleared her throat and asked the question that she'd been dying to ask: "Did Damien slouch?"

She'd expected Bobbie to be offended.

Instead, she laughed, a sound of joy, as if an old memory had struck her and brought back remembered happiness. "Who told you that?"

"Dr. Bari said I slouched like Damien."

Bobbie's face drooped, and she shook her head ruefully, "He never could say anything nice about my boyfriends."

"What happened to Damien?" Em asked. This was a crucial question. "Is he still alive? You didn't say."

"Damien died in a diving accident—drowned." Bobbie drew in a deep breath. She turned to look straight at Em, and there were tears in her eyes. "Ironic, isn't it? Either of us could have saved him if we'd been there." She turned away quickly and leaned back on the couch, stretching and letting her legs extend straight ahead.

Em nodded. She couldn't imagine drowning or not being able to help someone who was drowning.

Bobbie stayed stretched out, staring at the ceiling. It was a sort of stamped metal, dark with age. "That left me pregnant and without a boyfriend, much less a husband. In the depths of grief over his death, I was depressed. I had to call my brother for help. Max came and told me I had to let you be adopted."

"You let him decide my fate?" Em's voice was bitter. She shifted, moving farther away from Bobbie.

"Depression does strange things to people," Bobbie said. "I tried hard to believe what Max told me. I had to make it through those days." She sat up and looked directly at Em, holding up hands in appeal. "But he's been wrong all along. He said I had escaped a big burden, but I think I lost a lot of joy. He said it would let me bury the pain; but it just buried me in shame. I tried to forget you, but I couldn't stay away. I had to get glimpses of you someway. Do you remember playing t-ball? I watched a lot of your games."

"Really?" Doubt made Em shake her head.

Bobbie's voice grew excited. "Remember the game where you got five hits? And afterwards, your dad bought you chocolate ice cream at the snack bar, and you sat on the bleachers and ate it and watched your sister play her game. You were filthy with dirt and ice cream—" She looked away finally, her voice choked, but she forced out the last words. "—and you looked so beautiful."

Oh. But if this person was her mother and had loved her and followed her at a distance for years—if that was true, then so much time was lost to them. It couldn't be true. Bobbie didn't really care about Em. If she admitted that this woman loved her, then she also had to embrace the pain of separation for all those years.

"Why did you listen to him?" Em asked, her voice full of anguish.

Bobbie stood and paced in front of the bookcases. "He's my twin brother," she said simply.

Bobbie had a brother, Em thought. But Bobbie had denied Em any family. No. No. No.

She struggled to keep her voice level, but the rapid words spilled over, full of conviction, like a machine gun aimed with precision at Bobbie. "No. No, you're not my mother. Beth Tullis is my mother." With each statement, she emphasized the word, Tullis. "You might have given me life, but Beth Tullis has given me a soul. My father is Randall Tullis. My sister is Marisa Tullis. I am Emmeline Tullis."

Bobbie dropped her head into her hands in a gesture of despair.

But Em hardened her heart and kept talking. "I don't want you as my mother. I want to go home and never see you again."

Bobbie looked up, her eyes wide and full of tears. "You don't mean that."

Em turned away, refusing to look at her.

After a few moments, Bobbie rose and whispered, "I'm sorry."

Em heard Bobbie's footsteps, then the door shutting. Her heart ached and she wanted to fling open the door and run to her mother's arms. But she couldn't. Bobbie Fleming wasn't her mother.

Her name was Emmeline Tullis.

It wasn't Fleming. Not Fleming. Never Fleming.

Tullis.

PHOKE.NET

December 25

Dr. Mangot made a couple quick phone calls, trying to locate Em for Jake. "She's checked out of the hospital, though she has to stay in town for a couple weeks so we can monitor her. I don't know where she's staying."

Jake suspected that wasn't the whole truth, but he had no way to know for sure. "Who would know?"

"I'll check into it and get back to you."

Definitely a put off. But Jake had no way of searching for her himself.

While he worried about Em, Mom and Dad went into full diplomatic mode. They asked for their cell phones to be returned, but that was refused. Instead, they received a private office with a phone line to the mainland. Jake knew they'd be busy for hours. Mom would have to talk with the Risonian Embassy, with leaders who already supported them to make sure they didn't bail, and with leaders who opposed them to soothe the tensions raised by the Phoke's presence. Dad's Navy duties demanded that he first report in, and then allow a guide to show him around the city so he could give an eyewitness report to his superiors. Jake bet that the Pentagon was screaming for information after the Phoke announcement.

They kept the Phoke staff busy asking for paper and pencil, computers to work on, and passwords to log onto the Phoke Internet system.

Every phone call they made started with an explanation of their strangely high-pitched Tri-Mix voices.

One Phoke delivered a tray of steaming coffee and shortbread cookies. As the man was leaving, Jake asked, "Could I get a guide to show me around the city?"

"Of course," said the man.

"Do you mind if I tour the city?" Jake asked Mom.

She nodded her approval, barely looking up.

Jake followed the man, who looked exactly like the butler on that old British television show about the early 20th century, "Downton Abbey." Some of the girls at Bainbridge High

School had rediscovered the program and had binge-watched the whole six seasons. For a while, that's all they could talk about, so Jake had watched one or two episodes.

As he followed the man he now thought of as Mr. Carson, Jake tried to figure out how to find Em. He didn't trust Dr. Mangot to find Em for him, and even if she did, Jake didn't trust her to give him any information.

He thought back over the whole trip to Scotland: the aquarium and the octopus, diving with his friends to get his first glimpse of Aberforth Hills, and diving to the Nazi sub with mom, fighting General Puentes and being kidnapped by Captain Bulmer. Things had changed so fast. He'd come to Scotland with two goals. First, to support Mom and her ambassadorial duties. He was still learning how to be a Face of Rison. He'd gone to meetings with Mom and fought for his race's survival by arguing for transplanting their culture to Earth's oceans. He'd listened and grown. The Phoke may have put a nail in their coffin, as the American saying went, but he still had another goal: find Em. Fulfilling that goal might be possible.

She was here in Aberforth Hills. He had to find Em.

Mom and Dad would go to the cocktail party that evening to schmooze with the press from around the world. It was a tailor-made event for Mom to spread the word about the Risonian cause. So, he'd have hours before they worried about him again.

Mr. Carson took him to see the Gunby School and the City Hall. They were old and musty, another strike against the Phoke city and in favor of Risonian underwater cities. On Rison, they had old buildings, but they didn't stink from trying to keep out the ocean. Finally, Jake asked, "Where do the teenagers hang out?"

The man frowned disapprovingly. "Well, there are some clubs where bands play. My daughter's favorite band will be there this evening."

Jake took down an address, let Mr. Carson show him how to use an h-car, and at 8 pm, he walked into the Bog Myrtle. Sporting a low ceiling and stone floors, the congested cafe and bar throbbed with music and flickering lights. He recognized the band, The Phoke.

A girl dressed in a long flowing dress twirled by and was quickly swallowed up by the crowd. The light glinted from the granny-silver hair of a girl who danced alone. A bald guy swayed with a girl whose hair was so short that she was almost bald, too. Noise, people, crowds, constant movement—Jake hesitated, repelled by the crowd, as usual.

A hand slapped his shoulder. "Ah, it's the alien from Rison. What are you doing here?"

Looking up, Jake saw Enid Ways, the woman from the aquarium. Wryly, he thought, *I should've known she was Phoke.*

"Looking for my friend, Emmeline Tullis," he said loudly over the crowd noise. "But this city is overwhelming, so big." He used large gestures in case she couldn't hear him.

Enid leaned closer to his ear and quipped, "Well, failing means you're playing,"

Jake put his ear close to her ear. "Do you have any idea where I could look for Em?"

Enid put her arm through his elbow and mouthed, "Let's sit and talk."

Possessive, Jake thought. She was too old for him. Looking around the throng, though, she was the only friendly face. He nodded vigorously

They settled into a tiny booth away from the band, where they could talk at an almost-normal level. Enid leaned forward and said, "Your friend is here in Aberforth Hills? Have you checked the Phoke.net?"

"What's that?" Jake said.

"It's an Intranet that's only connected to servers in Aberforth Hills. It's got the most advanced security, of course," Enid said. "Couldn't let outsiders know we were here until we were ready."

She tapped on her phone and then looked up. "Emmeline Tullis was a patient at the Mangot Hospital. But she's been released."

"That's right," Jake agreed. "She's been very sick."

"Who's her doctor?"

"I think it was Dr. Mangot."

Enid voice went up an octave in excitement. "Oh! She's really good, the best! Such an inspiration! When I need to figure out how to get along up top, I call her. A great mentor!"

Jake thought of the cold, calculating doctor he'd met earlier. Maybe she only showed her good side to other Phoke.

A waitress stopped at their table. "Fish and chips for me," Enid said and raised her eyebrows at Jake.

"I'll have the same," he said, realizing that he was hungry.

For a moment, they listened to the band as a song crescendoed. In the cramped room, it sounded off-kilter, forced and harsh. "Why do you like this band?"

Enid's face shown with new enthusiasm. "Phoke in concert has a kind of off-the-cuff shagginess. Watch how the lead singer, Grady Tor, kind of goes into a trance with his lyrics."

Tor leaned over his guitar, eyes closed, head thrown back so that his Adam's apple bobbed as he crooned.

"I've heard this song a dozen times," Enid said, "and he never does it the same way twice. They add different instruments, too. Sometimes a mandolin or a violin. Sometimes a harmonica or a kazoo. Brilliant fun!"

"Brilliant," echoed Jake, but without enthusiasm. It was obvious he was out of place—or a fish out of water, as another American expression went. It was getting to be a bad habit, he realized, to constantly think in American slang. He brought the conversation back to Em. "So, can I get my own account on the Phoke.net? I'm good at research."

Enid shook her head. "Only Phoke have accounts and log in passwords."

"Could I use yours?"

"You're Risonian. My enemy." She tilted her head and studied him.

"Do you believe that?" Jake waved off the objection. "I know the octopus didn't like me, but do you dislike me, too?"

"You're an alien." She shrugged, like it was obvious.

Now Jake found his own passion rising, but even as he said them, he knew his words sounded mournful. "We don't want your cities. We just want to live. Our whole planet is about to be destroyed. You should understand our dilemma because it's so similar to your own. You'll be overrun with humans within a week. Will your Phoke culture survive that? You've barely survived when you've been hidden."

"We'll survive. For years, we've looked forward to this day. It was all planned."

He gulped. They were a well-oiled machine, everyone doing a pre-assigned task. "Humans and Phoke will have to figure out how to live in harmony. How easy will that be?"

The waitress delivered their food and for a minute they ate and thought. The Phoke band started a new song, and Enid sang along in between bites.

When the song ended, Enid said, "Tell me about Emmeline again."

"I met her in Seattle at a coffee shop. She swims amazingly fast, almost a state champion."

At Enid's blank stare, Jake expanded. "That just means she's the fastest in the state of Washington. Trust me, that's a big deal. She'll likely get college scholarships to be on someone's swim team. But she got sick, and they took her somewhere to be treated. And I've tracked her to Aberforth Hills and Dr. Mangot."

"What's your connection with Emmeline. Do you have a duty or something you have to fulfill?"

"Em is—well, my girlfriend."

Enid stirred her after-dinner coffee and looked skeptically at Jake. "You didn't sound so sure about that."

"She doesn't know who I am. The fact that the Risonian Ambassador is my mother was only announced nine days ago, the day after Em disappeared." Jake sat back and stared up at the string of lights over the dance floor. The band was taking a break now, so the room was full of noisy chatter, like a room full of crows, he thought. "I'd like to be the one to tell her that I'm an alien. I'd rather she not hear it from someone else."

Enid said, "I can see that."

"She thinks I can't even swim."

Enid raised an eyebrow again. "Ironic."

"I'm just a teenage boy looking for his girl," he said plaintively. It was a simple argument, but the only true one he had.

"A special teenage boy," Enid said.

"And a special teenage girl," Jake replied.

Enid stared at him as if trying to evaluate his intentions.

"Please," he said simply. "Help me."

Jake thought back to that argument with Em the first day they met. She had been so enthusiastic about the Bainbridge High swim team, trying to recruit him. Her eyes had been bright with excitement, and he told her that he was scared of the water. He couldn't believe he'd convinced her. It had almost ruined any chance he had with her, except that he was persistent.

The band struck up a new song, even shaggier than before, but with an almost familiar twang that made him turn to watch. It was a slow ballad, a story about a mermaid who pines away for a prince. Jake was sure that it had deep folk song roots, but the Phoke turned it upside down with an intricate melody line and melancholy harmony.

He turned to Enid and said with a quiet dignity, "Will you help me find Emmeline Tullis?"

Enid had been watching the Phoke play, too, but turned now and considered Jake. After a minute, she took a pen from her purse, and wrote on a napkin and shoved it across the table to him.

Jake read: EWays2015, Vulgaris

Of course. The password was the Latin name of common Atlantic octopus. Priscilla was Enid's darling.

He looked up to say, "Thank you." But Enid was on the dance floor with a tall guy.

Jake paid their bill and left excited. He hadn't found Em yet, but he'd found a way to try to track her across Aberforth Hills. She'd show up somewhere.

THE DAY AFTER

December 26
The day after Christmas was eerie. It was almost like the world held its breath for a day, trying to absorb the news that mermen and mermaids were real. And that they wanted to be called the Phoke. The media went crazy, but in spite of the Phoke's Contingency Plan, there was a huge vacuum of information. As predicted, though, the Phoke B&B was overwhelmed with traffic. The site went down twice overnight, but was quickly restored.

Mom worked almost endlessly. Ambassador Quad-de gave interviews—insisted upon the opportunity—to every news network who had crews in Aberforth Hills. After a while, Jake wondered if her smile was going to be permanently etched into her face. He sat in a few interviews with her to answer questions, but mostly they wanted the Risonian Ambassador's reaction to the presence of the Phoke.

She obliged them by providing video and photos of Rison. The Phoke media had put out lots of photos, so the news media compared Mom's photos of a Rison hospital with a Phoke hospital. They compared everything possible: hospitals, schools, sports centers, old houses, new houses, and city halls.

"Aberforth Hills is lovely," Mom said at the beginning of each interview. Sooner or later, though, she said, "Now that the Phoke have come out, and we know about them, I want to visit each of their cities and discover new vistas. I can't imagine losing your home town. Someday soon, I'll lose my whole planet. I only hope there will be some survivors to rebuild here on Earth."

Dad was interviewed endlessly, too. Commander Blake Rose was the Navy's only representative—actually, the only military from any country—so he had to give his appraisal of the city. He carefully avoided any discussion of the military readiness of Aberforth Hills because honestly, he hadn't had time to evaluate that.

When he wasn't being interviewed, he tried to communicate with ELLIS Headquarters. All anyone would say was that

General Puentes was at the hospital where his daughter, Captain Meryl Puentes, was recovering from a diving accident. Navy Headquarters, though, told him that ships were en route to the North Sea in anticipation of action from the ELLIS Forces.

Jake spent the day searching the Phoke.net for any signs of Em. He found nothing, so he walked through the tunnels till he found an h-car. With this simple transportation, he zipped around Aberforth Hills in hopes that he'd run into Em. Not likely. She was probably still recuperating somewhere and not going out. But he couldn't be still, a restless fear driving him. The only good thing was that after five times around the city, he was starting to understand its layout and remember how to get to different landmarks.

Still—no Em. No trace of Em after her hospital discharge.

Jake finally returned to the Mangot Hospital, exhausted and in despair.

Dinner for all the news crews and other guests was served in a large room set up as a dining hall. Buffet lines were along one wall, and staff circulated bringing drinks to the tables and later clearing away dishes.

Mom and Dad had already eaten, so Jake went to the dining room alone. His stomach was coiled into a knot, and he didn't know if he could eat anything. He'd left Rison to escape certain death. All he wanted was a chance to grow up, to fall in love, to work hard at a job he enjoyed, to enjoy an occasional vacation at the beach. He just wanted a life. Something most of his people would never have. He wanted to be given a chance to grow up. To become a man.

He wanted the future.

Dr. Mangot appeared at his table and motioned to a chair. "May I?"

He shrugged, and she sat.

Dr. Mangot asked, "Are you worried? Upset? You look tired."

Jake was very aware that every conversation he had while in the Phoke city was an important conversation. David would have known how to use all of this to gain a diplomatic edge, to help the Ambassador in her quest for their people. All Jake knew was to be honest.

"If I had a time machine," he said, "I'd go forward five months.

"Only five months? Not backward 100 years or forward 100 years?"

"No, why would I want to skip all of my life? I just want to know if I'm alone on this world, or if my fellow Risonians make it here. Will Swann, my Risonian father make it? I can face almost anything as long as the future includes my species. It won't be easy, we know that. But this one thing—will I be alone in the universe?—is crucial for me."

Dr. Mangot's jaw clenched. "I don't see a future for Risonians here. Earth's seas belong to the Phoke."

Jake's heart sank and despair washed over him, even as he admitted that Dr. Mangot was right. He pushed back his plate, sure now that he couldn't eat. He suddenly wished that he knew more of Risonian history. He wished he had memorized more Risonian poetry, had read more Risonian stories, had learned to play the traditional Risonian instruments. The *swifft* was a stringed instrument, the *bujo* was a wind instrument. Earth had its Bach and Beethoven; Rison had its Signs and Sup. He knew Risonian operas, he tried to encourage himself. But he had to admit that he only knew a dozen operas. And thousands had been written over the centuries. A whole culture lost. No, a world of cultures.

But even in his despair, he found another purpose, a deeper one. He might be losing a culture, but Earth had the chance to gain a culture, the Phoke. Em was gaining a culture and an ancestral home.

Dr. Mangot didn't know, and wouldn't believe even if he told her, but Jake was on the Phoke's side.

133

A TOLERABLE PLANET

December 26
Late on December 26, General Leroy Austin Puentes III sat on his bunk with his back against the wall. He was barefoot, and his knees were pulled up to support his tablet computer with its detachable keyboard. Yawning, he opened the messages app and texted his daughter, hoping that she'd be able to answer. When he'd heard about her diving accident, he took an emergency helicopter flight and spent 48 hours at her hospital bed. But last night—or was it early this morning?—he'd returned to work because—well, he was no good in a hospital room.

Besides, the Phoke's press conference on Christmas Day had shifted the balance of power in the Risonian negotiations, making everything more intense. Once he knew Meryl would survive, the General had to get back to his troops. He raised his shoulders up and let them fall, stiff and uncomfortable.

He texted:

Leroy: How R U feeling?
Meryl: Am pure done in. Finally have urinary control. Must try crutches today.

For a moment, Leroy's tears threatened to overflow, but he pushed them back and thought of Meryl's favorite quote from *Walden*, a book by the American environmentalist, Henry David Thoreau: "Heaven is under our feet as well as over our heads."

When she was recovered more, he'd take her—carry her if he had to—to their favorite bit of heaven on Earth, a forgotten stream in the tumbling hills of northern Scotland. And they would wade. They'd sit on the bank and dangle their feet in the clear, running water until they were so numb it almost hurt.

Leroy: How long on crutches?
Maria: Month? Maybe always. IDK.

Leroy: UR hearing? Will it come back?

Maria: IDK yet. Hearing aid tomorrow. Hope it's temp.

Leroy: SHARKS! I'll pay them back for this.

Maria didn't write back, and he understood. She'd always hated the Sharks, but now she was conflicted. She remembered enough of the DCS episode to know that she would've died without the Risonians. They went up top and got new tanks, and they kept her under to decompress as best they could. She wasn't sure, even, if the Ambassador's son had enticed her to stay under by chasing after an octopus.

Pah! Leroy was sure. That boy had deliberately compromised an experienced diver. And then made it look good by helping her survive. Leroy wanted to write back: What kind of life will it be? He'd rather be dead than deaf and crippled. He was glad that Gabby wasn't here to see their daughter in such bad shape.

But he only typed back:

Leroy: U can't trust someone who breathes H2O.

Meryl didn't text back.

Eventually, Leroy stretched, moaning at his aching muscles, and opened his tracking program. He wasn't sleeping well lately, waking too often through the night. Add to that the hospital vigil and he desperately wanted a nap. But not yet. It took a minute for the computer to fetch the GPS information from the nano trackers and when it finally displayed, Leroy was surprised. It placed Jake Rose in the middle of the North Sea.

Hunched over his computer, Leroy stifled another yawn. This situation needed his full attention, though, so he stood, stretched again, and found an energy drink in his small refrigerator. He popped the top and drank deeply. He was relying on them too much lately, but what else could he do?

He tried to remember details during the Sharks' brief visit to his yacht. Jake had only taken a sip of his tea, so he didn't have a full complement of nano-trackers. Maybe some of them had been expelled. But Edinburgh waste didn't wind up that far out to sea, did it?

136

To distract himself, Leroy turned on his satellite television. Of course, it was more of the Phoke nonsense. After that dramatic press conference on Christmas day, it would dominate coverage for a long time.

He glanced back at his tablet computer and made the connection. Jake Rose was in the Phoke city.

It finally made sense. This nonsense about mermaids and mermen was just a Risonian ruse. Their negotiations had fallen apart, and they weren't gaining the approval they needed to move a colony here. This Phoke stuff looked to Leroy like the Risonians have had secret installations for years. Now, they were trying to say that they were an indigenous species. Aye, right! What a load of crap. The Phoke were nothing more than Risonians pretending to be merpeople.

Every station was showing a news anchor reporting live from Aberforth Hills. Leroy saw through the publicity stunt. Surely, others would also. Earth would send the Risonians packing.

There was a knock on Leroy's door, and he opened it.

Captain Martinez handed him a sheet of paper. "Sir, here's that updated weather report you wanted." Martinez had been with Puentes for over ten years, a valuable aide.

Puentes read the report, while the Captain waited. The winter storm had quickened its pace and would hit their location about tomorrow, mid-morning. He had to make a decision soon.

"Your orders, sir? Do we go back to port?"

"Martinez, if you had a time machine, what would you do?"

"I don't know, sir."

"Well, I've thought about it a lot and I know exactly what I'd do." Puentes stood and rummaged about in a drawer while he talked. "I'd back up the world to November 16, 1974 and make sure the Aricebo message never got sent out into space. I'd blow up that rocket if I had to. If we didn't know anything about Rison, we wouldn't have soft-hearted idiots who want to rescue the Sharks, even though it will ruin Earth. It's crazy. If we save them, they'll be our death."

From the drawer, Puentes pulled out a pair of black socks. He sat on his bunk and started pulling them on. "That's why

137

we can't back off right now, in spite of the weather. I don't want to look back on this as a day we could have won, except we were cowards because of a little wind and snow."

The officer blinked at this outburst. "Yes, sir."

Puentes cleared his throat. "I still have to talk with the ELLIS Oversight Committee. I'll be on the bridge shortly with orders."

The officer saluted and turned to leave.

Leroy's computer messaging system pinged. He leapt to his tablet to see if it was Meryl. Instead, he saw a message from Karp. He was the Japanese Ambassador to the UN and head of the ELLIS Oversight Committee, Ambassador Karp Aylott:

Karp: How's Meryl?

Leroy: She'll make it. Thanks for asking.

Karp: You see the Aberforth Hills stuff?

Leroy: Is anyone on Earth not seeing it? It's brilliant PR.

Karp: It changes everything. If we already have an indigenous species that lives in the ocean, they'll have to be in on the negotiations.

Leroy: We need to destroy Aberforth Hills now, before the hoax goes any farther.

Karp: Hoax?

Leroy: Isn't it obvious? Risonians aren't getting the support they need, so now they are pretending to be Phoke. As an indigenous people, they would want a voice in what happens to the oceans. That hoax would put the Risonians into position to cast the deciding vote.

Karp: I hadn't thought of that. If it's a hoax, it's brilliant. That city looks really old. From the photos, I'd believe it's a 100-year-old city.

Leroy: Easy to fake.

Karp: True.

Leroy: So, what do we do, sir?

Karp: What do you suggest?

Leroy: Attack NOW. Expose the hoax. Capture leaders of the mythical Phoke and interrogate them. Force them to confess that they are really Risonians.

138

Karp: Hmmm. Let me talk with Kyle.

Kyle Burgeon was a career politician and the current US Ambassador to the United Nations. He was the other influential member of the ELLIS Oversight Committee. Most decisions were made by Kyle and Karp and rubber-stamped by the rest of the committee.

Leroy: Need to know soon. Within the hour. Winter storm in the North Sea will hit tomorrow morning. I can send in the submarine fleet, storm or no storm. But other boats need to go to safe harbor.

Leroy lay on his bunk and closed his eyes. He wouldn't sleep, just rest, he told himself. Indeed, he slept so lightly that when his computer's messaging system dinged again, he sat bolt upright. He dragged the computer to his lap and rubbed his eyes. Trying to focus, he read:

Karp: Submarine attack NOT approved. Must investigate Phoke to see if they are really indigenous or not. Move all vessels to safety. We'll talk more after the storm.

That was it. ELLIS understood nothing. Karp and Kyle were fools.

Leroy paced his tiny room, five steps one way, five steps back. Everything about the decision was wrong. The Risonians had fooled everyone with the Phoke ruse. They were taking Earth's own folk tales and using them to their advantage.

So. Karp and Kyle had made their decision, and now Leroy had to make his.

ELLIS is mine, he thought fiercely. These are my men, and they would follow me no matter what the officials said.

He upended his energy drink and drank the rest. He tossed the can into his trash can, where it clanged against other empty drink cans. It was an easy decision: attack.

Leroy would throw off the officials, though.

Leroy: Yes, sir. Right away, sir.

They wouldn't learn of his decision until the submarines didn't make it back to shore before the storm. And he made another decision: he'd take charge of one of the subs and lead the attack himself. From his bookshelf, he picked up Thoreau's *Familiar Letters*, a gift from Gabby when they married. It fell open to a well-worn passage: "What's the use of a fine house if you haven't got a tolerable planet to put it on?"

IRONIC STATISTICS

December 26
Face of Rison YouTube Channel
Most Popular Video: "Phoke, Risonians and Earthmen: The Possibility of Blue Planet Friendships"
Stats for December 26: 807 views

December 26
Jillian Lusk's YouTube Channel
Most Popular Video: "Blue Ball Flash Mob"
Stats for December 26: 192,492 views.

GONE ROGUE

December 27, 8:37 a.m.

"That's it," Commander Blake Rose said, clicking off his phone. "He's gone rogue."

The room stilled with the import of the statement. The Phoke military, along with the city officials and representatives of world news networks sat around a large table, drinking coffee and eating pastries. The conversation had been celebratory with everyone still excited by their announcement from two days ago on Christmas day, and all the coverage yesterday.

From the midst of the crowd, Dayexi's eyes were dark with worry. Blake wanted to reassure her, but too much was unknown. The last two days, she'd worked tirelessly to make sure the Rison position was heard: We want the Phoke people to come to the negotiation table, but they must do it quickly. Rison will implode soon.

Blake had helped when he could by getting her introductions to the few people she didn't already know, or by talking through how to approach this or that diplomat. They'd spent almost every waking moment together for the past two days. He'd had his own calls, investigations, and reports, of course, but he and Dayexi had shared an office and information. It was a rare gift for Blake. The Pentagon had ordered him to remain a neutral observer. So far, that had been easy.

Blake smiled at Dayexi's worried face, trying to wordlessly reassure her: "We're together in this. It will work out."

Captain Bulmer set down his coffee cup with a thump. BBC's female news anchor wore a purple sweater today. She was deep in conversation with Fox Suit, but stopped in mid-sentence. She snapped her fingers at the cameraman, who hoisted his camera to his shoulders.

Blake shook his head, and the cameraman reluctantly turned off his camera.

Blake explained that, to the best of their knowledge, General Puentes was now waging his own private war, and Aberforth Hills was his target. The U.S. Navy had enough intelligence in Scotland by now that they could monitor the ELLIS Forces fleet. The battleships had gone to harbor to avoid the winter storm. But the submarine fleet had gone dark, not responding to any communications.

The U.N. ELLIS Oversight Committee assured everyone that they had not approved any military maneuvers in the North Sea. But, they said reluctantly, they couldn't contact Puentes, either.

"We must assume that General Puentes means to attack. Today," concluded Blake.

Dr. Mangot was the first to respond, taking charge and issuing orders.

"We'll be moving now to our recording studio," she announced. "It was established so we could do remote medical consultations, so it's small. But as part of our Contingency Plan, we built in capability to accommodate two of the capable news anchors here." She held up a hand at the instant babble. "Wait. We'll try to work up a schedule so all of you get time. We can also accommodate remote feeds from multiple sources, so you can still broadcast even if you're not in the studio. If we're going to be under attack, I suggest you send cameramen out to strategic points."

She waved at two Phoke wearing Aberforth Hills t-shirts. "Van can help you pinpoint places for your cameras and get you set up. Mara will be in charge of the studio schedule. Please give her fifteen minutes to get it set up, and she'll take your requests in an orderly manner." Dr. Mangot barked the last few words as if she were a drill sergeant.

The hubbub subsided some.

She pointed to Purple Sweater and Fox Suit. "For now, you two come with me."

Purple Sweater smiled, but said, "Of course. The most important news scoop I've ever had, and I sound like a monkey. Any chance of normal air in the studio instead of Tri-Mix?"

Dr. Mangot rolled her eyes. To another Phoke, she ordered, "Find Dr. Bari and send him to the recording studio. Call his house. He's likely at home with his sister."

Corralling Captain Bulmer and her own security officers, Dr. Mangot moved to a side door and exited.

Blake hesitated, wanting to stop and discuss this new development with Dayexi. But she nodded at him to follow Dr. Mangot. "Later," she mouthed.

Blake detoured to pass by Dayexi, holding out a hand as he passed her. Briefly, she let her fingers trail against his. Blake felt that familiar tingle, and his heartbeat throbbed in his throat just as it had the first time they touched back on the Cadee Moon Base. It had been a lasting touch that had forged a friendship across the stars. It was a promise now: they weren't finished yet.

Without looking back, Blake followed Dr. Mangot. It appeared that the Phoke were organized and ready for almost anything. They'd had hundreds of years to imagine all the different scenarios, he supposed.

He didn't have much sympathy for General Puentes going rogue, but Puentes was walking into a hornet's nest. This invasion was going to be covered by worldwide media in a comprehensive way like never seen before. Puentes was going to be hit from every side in the media. Every side, except his own. There was no one to cover his point-of-view.

Thank goodness.

Blake caught up to Dr. Mangot and asked, "Do you have backup troops coming?"

"You want to know if we have a military," Dr. Mangot said flatly.

"Of course." Blake thought he might as well give it straight. "The Pentagon wants an evaluation."

"We've nothing to hide. Yes. Every Phoke town has a militia, sort of like the U.S.'s National Guard." She shook her head. "But no. They are capable of arriving anywhere on Earth within 48 hours, but we didn't account for Mother Nature. The winter storm will delay them. We can't count on help for at least three days, maybe four. What about the U.S. Navy?"

Blake scratched his head, worry making him shake his head. "Mother Nature. Three or four days."

They were on their own.

And the Pentagon expected him to remain neutral. He was forbidden to aid the Phoke in any way.

Blake had never disobeyed a direct order. But his family was here, Dayexi and Jake. He'd stay neutral as long as he could, but if they were threatened, he'd act. He wouldn't lose either of them just because Puentes decided to wage a private war.

THE NATATORIUM

December 27, 9:05 a.m.
Em stared up at the Michael Phelps Natatorium in amazement. One of the newest structures in Aberforth Hills, it was all metal and glass and lay at the northern edge of the city. Shelby had explained that glass strong enough to withstand the water pressure at this depth was relatively new.

Mid-morning was an odd time for people to exercise, so the lanes were empty. Shelby showed Em how to turn on the lights along the walls of the pool and turn off the overhead lights. The result was astounding. On the north side, the side of the pool was also the wall of the building, creating an observation area so that a swimmer could look out into the cold waters of the North Sea. Because the pool lay at the city's edge, light pollution wasn't bad. By reducing the light in the pool, Em could almost imagine that she was swimming in the deep sea.

"You'll be okay for a while?" Shelby asked. The natatorium was on the tourist's list of buildings, so his voice was squeaky from the Tri-Mix air. "I'm scheduled to visit cousins in South Africa in two weeks and have to get my vaccinations. And then I have to get my hair cut or my mom will scream." Today, instead of hospital scrubs, he wore a knit shirt that was tight on his arms and showed off his biceps.

"Why vaccinations?" she asked. Em didn't think she'd ever get used to the Tri-Mix cartoonish voices.

"I've never been out of England before. Just a precaution."

"Why are you going to South Africa now?"

"To visit cousins." Shelby hesitated, but shrugged and said, "Well, I'm also supposed to look for a Phoke girlfriend. They want us to marry other Phoke, but you know you can't just marry within one community or the gene pool goes bad." He waved a hand. "Parents are crazy. I'll marry whomever I want. But I won't turn down a trip out of the country. South Africa is in the height of summer right now."

Em wanted to laugh at how normal he sounded, like any of her classmates back in Bainbridge. "Take your time. Come back in an hour or two," Em said. "I won't overdo it or anything. I just want to try a couple laps."

"Sure, see you later. There are spare swimsuits in the dressing rooms. I left you some snacks and water in the bag if you need it. If I get delayed, just take a nap," he waved at the lounge chairs. "I'll be back later to take you home."

"Good idea. I am still getting tired—" she held up a hand to stop his protest "—and I'll take it easy. A nap would be good. So, take your time."

In the women's dressing room, Em grabbed a one-piece navy swimming suit from a stack and changed. She walked back out to the swimming pool and did a shallow racing dive into the pool. Lazily, she swam a lap, but then paused to gaze out the observation wall. She let herself sink underwater and hang there gazing into the North Sea. Someone had done landscaping—or seascaping—so that lovely corals clumped artistically on the sea floor. A variety of fish darted in and out of the area. She recognized a few such as haddock, lemon sole, and once a dogfish.

Em kicked lazily to the surface to catch a breath. Wait. She'd been underwater for over five minutes and hadn't been stressed for air at all. A quiet awe struck her, a sudden appreciation for the mermaid anatomy she had inherited. Imagine being 100% mermaid! Em was starting to relax into her Phoke body and let it do what came naturally. Her thinking had to change to keep up. She'd been trained to think as a human, that she could only stay underwater a minute or two, so she'd never tried for longer. She had to unlearn human limitations to learn how this one-quarter-Phoke body really operated.

She went under again, but when she came up, Em realized she was too tired to try again. She paddled slowly to the pool's side. She barely managed to pull herself out, awkward and stiff. She tottered to a lounge chair and collapsed. Wearily, she closed her eyes.

SEARCHING FOR EM

December 27

Jake was resting with his head on the table in front of him. Since they'd gotten the word about General Puentes going rogue, all was quiet. It was the proverbial calm before the storm.

Jake propped his phone on the table at eye level and turned it on. Em's photo was his screensaver, and he stared at her.

"Where are you?" he whispered.

If he'd felt an urgency to find her the last few days, it was overwhelming now. If she was here in Aberforth Hills when ELLIS attacked. . .

He shivered, not afraid for himself, but for Em. He had to find her.

The conference room doors flew open and in strode Colonels Lett and Barbena, followed by David and Jillian. They wore dark stretch pants, tennis shoes and dark t-shirts. The shirts had darker areas where they were wet. Likely, they had swim suits underneath, which meant they had just swum in.

Jake jumped up and yelled, "Finally!"

After the Contingency Plan press conference, Mom had asked the Embassy to send them in, quietly, coming underwater to avoid detection. Now, here they were with big grins.

Before he could say anything though, a loud ping resounded through the room. He whirled to look at the corner where the sonar station had been placed.

Another ping. Radar was hitting something. He thought sonar noises were only for the benefit of TV!

The sonar officer's voice rang out: "Sir, we have contact."

"What kind?" An officer in royal blue—the Aberforth Hills Militia—answered sharply.

"Lots of contact. Oh, no!"

"Report." The officer's voice was harsh, demanding.

"Sorry, sir. I'm counting fourteen targets heading our way. No. Sixteen, seventeen—They keep on coming. I don't know how many."

"How far away?"

"20 kilometers and closing fast."

Invasion!

Everyone started talking at once, and the quiet control room became a scene of chaos. The lights in the recording studio flared up as news crews started reporting live. Other new crews were recording feeds that would go out through the Internet. Still others made calls to check facts. The Risonian bodyguards were already beside the sonar panel where Mom, Dad and a couple men in Aberforth Militia uniforms were jabbing fingers at different targets.

Amid the noise, Jake turned back to his friends and motioned to the doorway. Since everyone was busy now with the impending ELLIS Forces attack, it was a good time to get away.

A moment later, the teens pushed through the doors and into the hallway. Jake clapped Jillian's back and shook David's hands. He wanted to crow with happiness. He swallowed hard, choking back emotion, surprised how relieved he felt when they walked into the room a few moments ago. "Wow, I'm glad to see you. About time you got here."

"We didn't get the same invitation you got!" David said with a wide grin. He nodded his chin to Jake. "What's up?"

"Em. I've got to find her before ELLIS gets here." Jake's fears were shredding his insides. Her illness was his fault, and it was his responsibility to make sure she was safe. She was only here in Aberforth Hills because of the *umjaadi* released when Dad's globe broke. She should be back in Seattle, far away from all this trouble. Far away from Puentes and his submarines.

"Where have you looked already?" Jillian asked.

Jake winced. "Too many places to name. But I've a couple new ideas. Her biological mother is Bobbie Fleming. Remember, she was the biologist who treated the sick harbor seals? Anyway, her brother is Dr. Max Bari."

At David's raised eyebrows, Jake nodded. "I know, it's weird. You saw him at the hospital? He brought Em here."

"Kidnapped her?" Jillian asked.

"No, they had a better hospital here for her illness. Anyway, I found his address here in Aberforth Hills. One of us can go there to look. The second place is Commander Bulmer's home. I understand his son, Shelby, has been giving Em tours."

Jake frowned at the thought of another guy showing Em around. "If you can each take one place, that would help." Jake pulled up the Phoke.net and showed them a map of the city and the best tunnel routes to each location.

"Where will you go?" David asked.

"The Phelps Natatorium, of course."

David and Jillian nodded in unison.

"Good idea," Jillian said. "If anyplace would appeal to Em, it's a swimming pool. Even if it's at the bottom of the ocean."

"Seriously?" David said. "The Phelps Natatorium. As in Michael?"

Jake shrugged. "Of course."

They all shook their heads at how obvious it was, once you knew.

"Here, take this. Just in case," Jillian said. She handed them both one of the flashlights they had used to swim out to Aberforth Hills.

"Good idea," David said.

No one stopped them as they raced down the hallways toward the lower exit. All doorways were now set to airlock in case the tunnels were compromised, so no water could enter the building. It took a few minutes to go through and find the hover cars.

"For now, our cell phones are still working," Jake said. "Call me if you find her."

GREEN LIGHT

December 27

"Sir, we're 20 kilometers away. They likely know we're coming now."

Puentes squinted through the tiny window of his sub, trying to catch a glimpse of the light from Aberforth Hills. Still too far out.

"General Puentes, sir, pull up your radar panel. It's a metropolis! We thought it would be a dozen structures, not hundreds."

Puentes checked his panel. The cutting-edge radar system was mapping the ocean floor before him. This far out, it was vague outlines, but with each passing minute, the map was adding details. In this first glimpse of Aberforth Hills, he was amazed at the size of the city. It was like a rabbit warren! How had the Risonians managed to create a community this large? It would take years. Could the Phoke story be real?

Puentes rubbed his tired eyes and took another sip of his energy drink.

It had to be Risonians. They'd had twenty years to bring people in, and for at least a dozen of the early years, ELLIS had few ways to track the Risonian spaceships. It was that long before Earth's technology caught up with their cloaking devices.

He tapped the display, and it said the city covered twenty square kilometers. He quickly searched and found that was roughly a fourth the size of the island of Manhattan. It wasn't just a few structures. Indeed, it was the size of a small city. The fact that they'd managed to keep it secret for decades was a miracle. But it also meant they were likely to have good defenses, something he hadn't counted on.

He gritted his teeth and considered. He had a fleet of 100 personal submarines, a huge investment of ELLIS Forces budget. And he didn't have official permission from the Oversight Committee. Karp and Kyle just didn't realize the danger of doing nothing. The Risonians lived in the water, and ELLIS had to fight in the water. That's why he'd pushed for the new subs. They were especially designed for underwater battles, with airlock doors so his men could exit to scuba for short time periods. The subs were also capable of acting as a decompression chamber if needed. They'd been training in the Mediterranean and had just brought the fleet to the North Sea for winter maneuvers. The timing couldn't have been better.

Even with the bigger city than expected, they had to attack. Surprise would be on their side today and never again. They had to quickly take Aberforth Hills out of any future discussion. At the very least, neutralize it.

It was now, or forever regret that you did nothing.

"Tell the fleet: Green light. Green light. I want an advance team out there with shoulder-fired missiles. Look for strategic targets. Power plants, communications. And you'd think they need air pumps from somewhere."

"Yes, sir."

Puentes was satisfied. ELLIS Forces were well trained and knew the limits of their equipment and gear. They wouldn't need much on-site direction. That left the question: what would he do?

He opened a new channel to Captain Martinez. "When the action starts, you're with me. We're going hunting for hostages."

THE LION'S MANE

December 27

Jake's path to the Natatorium went east for half a mile before he reached a major intersection where he followed signs and turned north. The swimming center was at the north end of Aberforth Hills.

In the distance, he heard explosions. The ELLIS invasion had started.

Suddenly, behind him, an explosion shattered the tunnel and cold water poured in. Jake realized he couldn't outrun the stream of water, so he jumped off the hover car and let the rush of water carry it away. It only took a second for his water breathing to kick in. At this depth, the water pressure was enough to keep human divers from staying submerged long, but it didn't bother Jake's Risonian anatomy. He lifted his arms to allow his gills to breathe deeply and tried to decide what to do. Should he stay in the tunnel, or exit to swim to the natatorium? He'd likely find a moon pool near the natatorium, which would allow him to enter the tunnels if needed. And every building had emergency airlock entrances.

Another explosion sounded near him; the tunnels were being targeted by ELLIS. Then it made sense to get out of them.

But the onslaught of water was pushing him away from the hole in the tunnel. No sense in fighting it if he didn't have to.

Jake paused, taking advantage of a quiet eddy near a tunnel that was just starting to fill with water. He put on the forehead flashlight and stripped off his sweat pants, leaving him in just swim shorts that he'd worn ever since he got here. Finally ready, he let the tide of rising water carry him along until he came to another intersection, and it had a moon pool. Of course, with the tunnel filling up, water frothed up from the moon pool, too. He dove cleanly through the froth and came up in the cold ocean water at about 90 meters deep. A slight chill swept over him, but his magma-sapiens blood quickly adapted to the temperature.

He took a moment to orient himself.

To the south, he saw regular flashes from underwater missiles. ELLIS was searching for military targets that would cripple the city. If Dr. Mangot was correct, most important systems were embedded below the structures. You'd have to blow up the whole Mangot Hospital before its generator stopped.

Jake could do nothing to help anyone. Except maybe Em.

He zipped his legs into a tail and kicked toward the distant natatorium. It was a silvery white metal and looked like the square chest his grandmother, Easter, used to store her quilts and keepsakes.

Suddenly, he stopped still. He'd been daydreaming, so he was unsure what had startled him. But some instinct told him to stop.

Ahead, it looked like pieces of kelp or other seaweed had been torn free by the storms up top. Lifting his left hand, he brushed away one strand. Reflexively, he jerked back and cradled his left arm with his right. Pain shot up his arm to his elbow and then traveled slowly toward his shoulder.

Panicked, he twisted, trying to figure out what had hurt him.

Another strand of seaweed grazed his neck, and suddenly he was bending double in pain. He forced himself to lift his head enough to try to find the source of the strands.

There.

A jellyfish. Not seaweed, but a jellyfish tentacle. It had stung him and would sting again if he touched another tentacle.

In his dim flashlight, the creature was a golden half-sphere at least five feet across with very long tentacles trailing away, like a massive shrub with thousands of tiny branches coming out of the dome. Tentacles, some perhaps a 100 feet long, floated all around him. The jellyfish's head was about Jake's height. Using his leg-tail to make powerful strokes, he backed away quickly. As the jellyfish flexed, it looked like a golden flower with eight lobes. Right under the hood was a mass of hair-like tentacles that resembled a lion's mane. It was a lion's mane jellyfish and because its tentacles were so long, it was one of the longest animals on Earth. Rare at this depth, it had likely pushed down to escape the winter storms above.

It was also poisonous. How would his Risonian anatomy react? Jake would know soon enough.

He hung immobile, letting the giant jellyfish drift away. Meanwhile the pain from the stings spread up his arm and down from his neck until waves of agony made him almost unaware of his surroundings. Suddenly, Jake felt as if he needed air, needed to breathe. He rubbed a hand across his underarm gills and realized that they were clamped tight with a muscle spasm. He couldn't water-breathe.

He tried to ignore the spreading pain and tried not to panic. He needed a moon pool and a tunnel with air. Agitated, Jake swept his gaze around, looking for a solution. Nearby tunnels were flooded, and that wouldn't help.

There, in the distance, he saw the shiny natatorium. And there was the usual red arrow pointing to a moon pool. He had a few minutes before he ran out of air. His body would automatically shut down all non-essential functions to reduce the need for oxygen. Move, he told himself. Move.

With weak tail thrusts and clumsy arm strokes with his numb arm, Jake made for the arrow. He grimaced at the pain, feeling himself grow even clumsier as the numbness spread.

But he swam.

The jellyfish's sting had left a blister on his left hand, and his awkward strokes made it burst open, sending sharp stabs through that hand.

Still, he swam.

The cold reached into his body until his bones ached. He realized that because he was oxygen-starved, his body's magma-sapiens warming couldn't kick in. If he didn't make the moon pool soon, he didn't know whether he'd drown or freeze first.

On and on, he swam.

The thing that bothered him was that he might never see Em again. The very idea frightened him, so he thrashed harder through the water. He wanted to watch her taste haggis, and listen to her sing Happy Birthday to him, and swim beside her in a tropical sea.

He wanted to kiss her.

Life was too short to waste by dying in a frigid Northern sea on a planet called Earth.

He s-w-a-m.

It could've been five minutes or five hours.

All he knew was that a red arrow was above him.

Why had he fought to get here?

Where was Em?

Down. He obeyed the arrow and dropped down. He hovered a moment.

He needed air.

He gave one last thrust of his tail.

JAKE AND EM

December 27

Jake shivered. His eyes fluttered open. He lay half in and half out of a moon pool.

He groaned and pulled himself out onto the side of the pool. Rolling awkwardly to his back, he stared up at the roof of the tunnel. His lungs expanded, sucking in a deep breath.

Jake held up his hand and stared at the ragged skin around the jellyfish's blister. This was crucial information that he needed to give to his mother. The sting of a lion's mane jellyfish had shut down his water breathing. If their enemies learned this, they'd analyze the chemicals in the jellyfish's sting to use as a weapon against the Risonians. They could use it as a poison dart or simply contaminate a section of water with it. The *umjaadi* infected Earth's Phoke, and the lion's mane jellyfish could drown Risonians. It seemed symmetrical, somehow.

A sudden explosion shook the tunnel. Puentes was still attacking!

Jake struggled to sit up, shoving with his right hand to gain his balance. He had to find Em.

Jake staggered to his feet, got his bearing and realized he was right beside the natatorium. He lurched to the door and leaned against it as he punched the air lock controls. The door slid open with a squeaky rasp. He stepped inside and punched more buttons. A few moment later, he stepped out—more steady now—into the lobby of the natatorium. The smell of chlorine hit him. A shudder of revulsion ran up his spine. Em had told him they had to use chemicals because people peed in the water, and there was no way to keep it sanitary without the chemicals. Gross.

He pushed through a door into the pool room and let it slam behind him. There was an Olympic-sized pool, and there, on a lounge chair, was Em. Finally.

≋ ≋ ≋

A door slammed. Em woke with a start. That would be Shelby returning, she thought sleepily, and opened her eyes. Instead, right in front of her was Jake Rose.

Her heart suddenly beat frantically, and she tried to catch her breath. Jake!

He wore a long sleeveless t-shirt over swim shorts. He was dripping water onto the floor.

He tapped out a message on his phone, then turned to her. "Em! I've been frantic to find you after the note you left me in your bedroom back home. Are you OK?"

Jake's voice was squeaky from the Tri-Mix air, but it was music to Em's ears. Involuntarily, she yawned. She was still so tired. But seeing him lit up her heart.

She struggled to sit up. Stretching her arms upward, she shrugged. "Turns out, I didn't need to be rescued. But why are you here? Do you even know where you are?" Jake looked pale and tired himself. Was he OK?

Jake's face split into a big grin, and he sank to the floor beside her chair. "Aberforth Hills, home of the Phoke. Or the Mer Folk. Mermaids, Mermen. Or whatever you want to call them. With the big Christmas announcement, everyone on the planet knows about this place."

She nodded, glad that she didn't have to spend energy explaining things.

Suddenly, he seemed shy. "I, um, have something I need to discuss. You've been sick, right? So did you see any news reports since you were kidnapped?"

"Not kidnapped? Medical evacuation."

"Yes. Right. Medical evacuation." His right hand was rubbing the side of his left hand in a nervous gesture. "Since then, have you seen many news reports?"

"No. I was knocked out for a couple days and weak for several more days, sleeping a lot. I've just been cleared to move around some, but I can't leave Aberforth Hills for another month."

"So-o-o-o, you haven't seen my news?"

She shook her head, curious. "Tell me."

Jake leaned back on his hands and stared up at the ceiling of the natatorium. With his head back, she saw red whelp on his neck, and almost asked about it. But he pulled his knees to his chest and hugged them.

He's embarrassed. What could be so hard to tell me? she wondered.

Still without looking at her, Jake said, "You know how I said I couldn't swim? That's not exactly true." Now, he did glance over at her.

It struck her! "You're Phoke! So am I! My mom is a mermaid, although my father was Japanese-American."

Jake leaned forward with his legs crossed, and frowned. Why hadn't Dr. Mangot told him this important information? She'd deliberately withheld it.

"You're half-Phoke?" he said. "Oh. That's why you're here in Aberforth Hills."

"A quarter-Phoke," Em corrected. Then, she hesitated, quivering. In her excitement, had she misread what he was saying? "And you're Phoke, too, right?"

"How do you know you're Phoke? Who are your parents?"

"Bobbie Fleming, the biologist. She's half Phoke. Obviously, that's why she's a marine biologist."

Jake nodded. "Makes sense. I thought I saw her twice in Edinburgh. She must have done some shopping before coming down to Aberforth Hills. And your father?"

"A Japanese-American. He died in a diving accident. In any case, Bobbie had already put me up for adoption." Her eyes narrowed and she repeated, "And you're Phoke, too, right?"

Jake's eyes were big with worry, and he lifted his chest and held himself rigid. His voice was low, but defiant. "I'm Risonian. My mom is Dayexi Quad-de, the Risonian Ambassador."

"Oh." Em was stunned. Alien. From Rison. Oh.

One of those.

Then, angrily, she demanded. "Show me."

He lifted his arms, and instead of a hairy armpit, there were parallel lines of a gill. She started up, standing to get away from him. He shoved up heavily and followed her.

They were at the edge of the pool, but she backed away again, shaking her head in denial. "No."

Jake kept his arm up, as if he had to prove his words. He needed her to understand that they had so much in common.

"No," she yelled at him. "NO!"

161

"Yes," Jake said and stepped closer.

She shoved him into the water, angry that he'd lied to her all those months, and angry that—oh, she didn't know—angry that he could probably out swim her, even though she was a quarter-Phoke. Angry at all the time wasted by both of them denying who they were. Her head whirled in sudden dizziness.

Jake bobbed back up to the surface, and his eyes locked on hers. They were dark eyes, full of sadness and hope and—oh, she didn't know. She might have resisted him, but he reached up to her, his hands stretched in a wordless appeal.

They were worlds apart and yet that yearning look on his face—her breath caught and her heart hammered. She sat on the pool's side and leaned over to let him take her hands, to let him gently pull her into the warm pool, to let him draw her down to the observation glass. For long minutes they hovered, admiring the beauty of Earth's cold sea depths, his warm hand refusing to turn loose of hers. A sand eel squirmed through the seaweed. Behind a rock, a crab scuttled. A flat fish that she didn't recognize squirmed to hide in the sediment of the sea floor. There was a kinship, something that connected them, even though they were from opposite sides of the galaxy. Here, under the water, they were almost the same sort of creature. Almost.

Finally, Em pointed upward: she had to breathe.

He caught her around the waist, holding her lightly; facing each other, they slowly rose. Em's heart pounded at his touch, his nearness. When they broke the surface, she breathed easily a couple times, shocked that she didn't have to gasp for air after being submerged for so long. Her dark hair clung to her face and neck and shoulder, and it tickled her face. Jake's hand reached gently to push the hair behind her ears. Then, he leaned closer.

This was it. They had almost kissed at her parent's mountain cabin near Mt. Rainier when the volcano threatened to erupt. But her sister and her boyfriend had interrupted them. This time, no one else was around.

Jake's arm tightened on her waist, pulling her closer.

A door banged.

Em's head jerked around, and she pushed away from Jake, disappointed, aching to be back in his arms.

David and Jillian strode into the room calling, "Em! Jake!"

Em raised a hand and called, "I'm here."

David and Jillian trotted along the side of the pool till they neared her. Suddenly weak, Em allowed Jake to help her to the pool's side, and allowed David and Jillian to pull her out.

Then, the door slammed again, and a blond guy appeared.

Quickly, Em introduced him. "Jake, this is Shelby Bulmer. Shelby, do you know Jake Rose?"

"The Risonian ambassador's son," Shelby said flatly. "Everyone on the planet knows him."

"Are you Commander Bulmer's son?" Jake asked, in an equally noncommittal voice.

"Yes."

"He's the officer who kidnapped my mother and me."

"He does his duty." Shelby spread his stance to balance on the balls of his feet, ready—just in case.

Afraid they'd start fighting, Em introduced Jillian and David as Jake's friends.

Em pushed herself up to stand, awkward and uncertain. She stumbled to a poolside lounge chair and dropped onto it. She lay back and closed her eyes.

Instantly, Shelby and Jake were beside her.

Shelby said, "I told you not to over do it!"

Jake said, "Em, what do you need? What can I get for you?"

Em smiled, flattered that two boys were fussing over her. "I'm fine. I just need to rest a while. Find chairs and sit, and we'll just talk for a while."

RISON V. PHOKE ANATOMY

December 27

Em stretched out wearily on the lounge chair. Still tired from the jellyfish poisoning, Jake lay back on his own lounge chair. Shelby, though, pulled up a short chair and sat upright near the foot of Em's chair where he had a good view of her face.

David and Jillian, though were fascinated by the observation wall.

"Can we take a quick look?" asked Jillian.

"You're not dressed for it," Jake said.

Shelby said, "There are always spare swim suits in the dressing rooms. They can use whatever they find."

"It'll have to a be a quick look," Jake said. "After all, humans can't stay underwater as long as Risonians or Phoke."

Jillian rolled her eyes, but went to the women's dressing room, while David pushed through the door to the men's dressing room. They were back out shortly and dove into the water together.

In a reasonable voice, Jake said, "You know, Shelby, we should try to be friends. Risonians and Phoke should be allies because we're both aquatic." It was hard for him to extend an offer of friendship, but Jake was trying hard to be more diplomatic like his mother.

Shelby shook his head, his blond hair so different from Jake's dark curly hair. "The Phoke may wind up friends with Risonians. But I'll always remember that I'm an Earthling first, a water creature second."

"Do you think the world is going to just let the Phoke come out and actually have a say in anything?" Jake asked scornfully. He was skeptical about any politician giving up power. "Wouldn't it be better to ally with the other water creature who will inhabit your oceans?"

Shelby said scornfully, "Risonians aren't even mammals! They're half-fish."

"Are Phoke mammals?" Jake asked. He hadn't thought about this biological distinction before. Risonians wouldn't fall under Earth's definition of mammal or fish. They were a different class of creature.

"Yes!" Shelby said. "Mammals breathe air, give birth live, give milk to their babies, and have hair. We are kin to whales and dolphins. We don't have gills."

Jake thought about the Mer anatomy. They weren't truly water creatures. They were air breathers with an anatomical adaptation that let them stay under water for long periods. But they weren't like Risonians who could breathe either water or air and stay under as long as they wanted or needed.

He remembered going to his grandparents' house in Sobey, a city in the Chi-Chi Sea, just south of Tizzalura's shores. His grandmother, Grace Quad-de usually had long, plaited hair, but at night, she loosed her hair, and he remembered her hands, spotted with age, combing through her hair and scratching her head. Laughing, she said, "When it's braided, it pulls so tight that it itches. I have to let it down at night."

Their home was open to the ocean currents, so her long white curls floated around her head giving her an ethereal look, delicate and ageless.

Jake loved his bedroom there—Swann's bedroom as a child—where fresh water coursed over him all night long. It was the best sleep.

But the Phoke didn't have the anatomical structures to be true water creatures. He almost pitied them. They could just dive for an hour, maybe two. Those who were only half-Phoke, maybe even a shorter time. They'd never know the comfort of an ocean breeze rocking you to sleep.

"Kin to whales. Fascinating," Jake said. "How can you live under water then?"

Em spoke up. "I think I know part of that answer. Dr. Mangot told me that the Phoke have a different anatomy. Our ribs hinge at the spine, which lets the chest walls collapse at the high water pressure, like at this depth. If I exited a building while at this depth—" She waved at the observation wall and the sea beyond. "—I could do it, but moving suddenly into that level of pressure would mean the immediate collapse of my ribs, which could hurt." She signed and closed her eyes.

Shelby continued, "In the early days of Aberforth Hills, that was the only way to go from building to building. But we quickly invested in a tunnel system, so you don't have to go outside to move to a different building. We can do it; we just don't like doing it at this depth."

"I didn't know you had hinged ribs!" Jake said. "What other anatomical differences are there?"

Em kept her eyes shut and waved at Shelby to explain.

Shelby said, "When the rib cage collapses, the air is compressed into the upper part of the trachea, and into special air chambers where it can't be absorbed into the lungs. That way we don't absorb oxygen, but we also don't absorb nitrogen, which causes the bends. Our muscles use less oxygen, too, and some peripheral systems are shut down. When we're diving, we don't digest food, for example."

"Interesting," Jake said. "Our bodies are also extremely efficient at lower water depths. Must be a similar adaptation."

"If we stay down long," Shelby said, "Our heart rate slows."

"Now there we're different. Risonian heartbeats get faster at depths, keeping us warm. What we call the magma-sapiens response."

Shelby nodded. "Named for the volcanoes."

Jake nodded. He sat up to take a quick look at Em's face which was too pale, frowned and leaned back again. At least she was resting now. But it wasn't good that she tired so easily. He wondered what would've happened if David and Jillian hadn't interrupted them.

"Yes, the volcanoes. The reason the Risonians must come to Earth—or die," he answered Shelby. "Does it bother you at all that a whole planet may be destroyed, along with and every living thing on it?"

"Of course, we care. But the cost is extremely high. If Risonians contaminate our oceans with foreign organisms, it could kill the Phoke. Doesn't it bother you that your very presence threatens a race of people on Earth?"

"Of course—" Jake started.

But Em interrupted, "Those organisms made me very sick. And Dr. Mangot warns me that I could relapse at any time. They don't know the real course of the disease."

Jake said nothing, for what could he say? She was right. It was the Risonian's fault that she was sick and the Phoke were threatened. Em was sick from an organism from his home world of Rison that his father had accidentally released into the ocean. Guilt struck him hard in the gut. But what could he do? Rison was going to implode. And soon.

Em sighed softly.

Looking over, Jake saw her breathing had slowed, and her mouth was slightly open. She'd gone to sleep. With her eyes closed, her dark lashes looked longer than ever. He wasn't really surprised that she was a mermaid, for she'd always been his siren. He couldn't imagine a world where she didn't exist.

Suddenly, a fierce emotion gripped him, and a terrible resolve built within him. Dr. Mangot said the only way to find a cure was to go to Rison. He had to be on that medical mission team. "I promise, Em," he vowed silently. "I'll find you a cure."

There was no answer. He looked closer at Em. No, she wasn't asleep, she had passed out.

ANEMIC

December 27

"Em, we're talking to you," Jake reached over to shake her slightly. Her head lolled to the side.

Shelby stepped forward threateningly. "Leave her alone."

Jake shook his head. "You don't understand. Em's not asleep." He sat up now and gently shook her shoulders. "She's passed out."

Shelby's eyes widened in shock. Anxiously, he knelt on Em's other side and patted her hand. "Em. Wake up."

"How sick is she?" Jake asked grimly.

"Don't know." Shelby sat back on his heels. His forehead furrowed with worry. "Dr. Mangot said she could relapse at any time."

Jake pulled out his phone, glad once again that it was waterproof. He dialed Mom's number and quickly explained that Em was sick. Mom passed her phone to Dr. Mangot.

"She's unconscious?" Dr. Mangot's voice was calm, almost cold.

"Yes," Jake said.

"I need you to check if she's anemic. Here's what you do. Gently pull down the bottom eyelid. It will look pale at first, but then it should pink up."

"She's half-Japanese and half-Phoke. Will it still work for her?"

"Yes. Hurry."

By now, Jillian and David were kneeling beside Em's lounge chair. Jake knelt beside Em and handed the phone to Jillian. "Talk to her while I do this."

With great care, like he was handling a breakable porcelain doll, Jake pulled down her eyelid. It was pale, as expected. And it stayed pale.

Jake took back the phone. "Anemic."

Dr. Mangot said, "Probably severely anemic. The *umjaadi* is interfering with her body making blood. She needs a transfusion. Immediately. What's your blood type?"

"Um, half Risonian."

"Oh, yeah. Who else is there?"

Jake glanced at Jillian and David with a frown. He held a hand over the phone and said, "She wants to know your blood types."

Jillian stared blankly, but David stepped in smoothly, "We're both A negative."

Jake raised an eyebrow, but said into the phone. "Jillian and David are A negative."

"That won't work," Dr. Mangot said. "Em is type B."

"We need B blood type," Jake repeated to the others.

Shelby stepped forward, "My blood is B."

Jake reported that to Dr. Mangot, who asked, "Did he get those vaccinations this morning like he was scheduled for?"

Jake relayed the question.

"Yes," Shelby said. "Does that matter?"

Dr. Mangot was adamant: "That would be like giving a sick person a vaccination. You'd force her immune system to respond to the vaccinations, which could overload her system. We need someone else."

"Who?" asked Jake.

Angrily, Dr. Mangot said, "I used my blood for her three days, so I can't do it again."

Jake realized there was only one logical person. Em would be furious, but she had to have compatible blood and she needed it now. "Try Em's mother, Bobbie Fleming."

Dr. Mangot said, "Oh, of course. She's in the safe room under the school. It's hard to reach them there. A lot of the attack is centered around the Gunby clock because it's such a tall landmark. OK. Look, I'll try to get hold of her and get her over there. I'm on my way."

Jake hung up, worried. With the city under attack, would Ms. Fleming be able to make it to the natatorium?

Shelby growled (as much as you can growl with Tri-Mix), "Em doesn't want to see her birth mother. She won't like this."

Jake understood why Em didn't want anything to do with Bobbie Fleming. It made sense to dislike the person who gave you away to strangers. Rejection like that deserved rejection in return. But Em had to have blood, and blood relatives were the most likely matches. Em was in no position to refuse.

THE ENEMY IN THE NATATORIUM

December 27

The natatorium was too quiet, too calm. The hum of the swimming pool's pump was a white noise that made Jake groggy. He lay in a lounge chair next to Em's and stretched out his hand toward hers, but she was still passed out. He closed his eyes. The past few hours had been so full, along with his jellyfish injuries, that he was exhausted. He hoped Dr. Mangot would get here fast, but till then, he could do nothing more.

Apparently, Shelby was restless. Jake heard the blare of music and peeked at what was happening. Jillian, David and Shelby were hunched over Shelby's phone.

"What are you watching?" Jake asked.

"You won't believe this," Jillian said. "The Phoke are broadcasting the battle live. You can see the subs circling in and divers with bazookas—or whatever they are."

Reluctantly, Jake sat up and went to bend over Shelby's back so he could see the screen, too.

The scene showed the bird's eye view of Aberforth Hills—probably the camera from the top of Mangot Hospital. It cut to the scene of a diver with a shoulder-held missile launcher. It fired. The missile spun through the water and BAM! A section of the tunnels exploded.

Meanwhile, missiles streaked away from the city, exploding amidst submarines. It was impossible to tell who was winning.

A doorway banged, and the teens whirled in alarm.

Dr. Mangot strode purposefully toward them, holding a couple cases of medical gear. Her thick hair was braided down her back, and she wore the blue camouflage gear of the Aberforth Militia. "Where is she?"

Jake motioned toward Em. Dr. Mangot dropped the bag, sat on the lounge chair that Jake had been using and reached for Em's wrist. She paused, apparently counting heartbeats. She looked up in alarm.

"What's wrong?" Jake was suddenly cold and started shaking. "What's wrong?" he asked again, louder.

Dr. Mangot's words were staccato-like: "I checked the hospital records, and it turns out I had blood samples for Dr. Bari and for Em. They don't match. I'm sure there are many more matches in Aberforth Hills, but I don't have those records, and there's no time to screen people. The only matches with the records I had were Shelby and Bobbie Fleming. Since Shelby got those shots this morning, I'd rather not use his unless we have to."

"Where's Ms. Fleming?" Jillian asked. She and David had stepped up to flank Jake, David gripping Jake's shoulder.

Jake felt their support and was glad for it. Without his friends, he would be totally distraught.

"Ms. Fleming has been helping protect the kids at the Gunby School. I talked to her, though, and she's going to try to make it." Dr. Mangot hesitated. "But there's fighting between here and the school. I had to take a round-about route myself. To get here, she might have to swim. In spite of being half-Phoke, she's never been comfortable doing that at this depth."

"But she's going to try?" Jake insisted.

"She's on her way." Dr. Mangot put the back of her hand on Em's forehead. "At least there's no temperature."

The natatorium door was flung open again. Jake spun around, expecting Bobbie Fleming.

Instead, General Puentes stood just inside the door, flanked by another ELLIS officer. With a childish Tri-Mix voice, Puentes said, "Finally. I'll have the hostages I need."

Dr. Mangot stood and strode toward Puentes. "This is a medical emergency situation. According to the Geneva Convention's rules of engagement—"

"You're in my way."

Dr. Mangot stood with her feet spread and hands on her hips.

"That's right," she said.

"You go on and take care of the girl. I can see she needs you," Puentes said placidly.

Reluctantly, Dr. Mangot swiveled to look at Em.

Puentes shoved the Dr. Mangot to the floor and trotted forward a couple steps. He cocked his gun, aimed at Jake, and pulled—

Just in time, the other ELLIS office knocked his gun down, so that Puentes couldn't pull the trigger.

Puentes jerked his gun away and glared at the officer.

"You can't shoot in here, sir. If you puncture the wall, it will depressurize and water will break the walls," the officer said calmly.

"Martinez, you may be right," Puentes voice was harsh with rage. "But never touch my gun again."

"Yes, sir. Sorry, sir." Martinez said calmly. He nodded toward the teens. "We can take them with knives, anyway."

The ELLIS men had stripped off the bulky diving suits somewhere else and only wore thin black wetsuits without hoods. Heavy belts held an assortment of gear. Both men set down their weapon and pulled wicked looking knives from their belts.

Jake and the others shoved lounge chairs to block Puentes and Martinez. Then the teens retreated, putting several more rows of chairs between them.

"You'll have to catch us first," Jake said. He didn't mind a good knife fight, but he didn't have his Risonian knives on him. And there was Em to think of. It was probably best to avoid a fight, if possible.

Dr. Mangot had risen and gave the soldiers a wide berth to make it back to Em. Looking down, she shook her head. "It looks bad. We don't dare wait." She opened her case and started pulling out equipment. "Shelby, get over here. We don't have a choice."

White-faced and reluctant, Shelby skirted a couple lounge chairs and sat on the one next to Em. The doctor ripped open a small foil packet and pulled out an alcohol pad. She nodded her chin toward Shelby's sleeve and he understood. He pulled it up exposing the inside of his elbow. Dr. Mangot swabbed his arm with the alcohol pad.

The soldiers avoided the area where Dr. Mangot was working but advanced toward the other teens. Suddenly, Martinez reared back and threw his knife at Jake.

Jake saw the motion from the corner of his eye and instinctively ducked.

The knife clattered on the tile floor. Jake scrambled after it and picked it up. Now the fight was fairer. It was three against two, but each side had a knife now.

Except Martinez pulled out a spare knife.

No matter, Jake thought. He had one goal: to give Dr. Mangot time for Em's blood transfusion. That meant they had to distract Puentes and Martinez.

He decided to attack just long enough for the men to give chase. He darted toward Martinez, but at the last minute, he turned and tried to slash Puentes.

Instinctively, Puentes lifted his arm in self-defense.

Jake crowed when the knife bit through Puente's wetsuit.

It was barely a scratch, but it made Puentes mad. His expression was angry before, but now his chin was set, and his eyes flared with fury. "Why, you little—"

He took the bait and lunged toward Jake.

But Jake was backing up toward the exit, trying to keep the ELLIS men away from Dr. Mangot.

David dashed in and executed a perfect soccer slide-tackle on Martinez. They went down in a heap, allowing Jillian to dart in and chop at Martinez's arm, making him drop his second knife.

But Martinez was a seasoned soldier. He flipped David and scrambled for the knife. Jillian kicked it, making the knife fly toward the water.

They all rose and stared at each other, wary. Martinez shrugged. Reaching for his back, he pulled a third knife and waved it menacingly toward David and Jillian.

Meanwhile, Puentes attacked Jake, charging so quickly that Jake couldn't side-step. They grappled. Jake's hands couldn't find purchase on the slick wet suit, but Puentes easily grabbed Jake's arm.

Jake stepped into Puentes, shifting his balance, and expertly jerked Puentes up and over his head to slam him to the floor.

Jake smiled grimly. They were winning, in spite of their youth and inexperience.

Suddenly, the door banged open again.

Someone rushed in, dripping wet. Everyone turned to stare. The figure—a woman—bent her head and flipped her long hair to her back. Bobbie Fleming's chest swelled, and she stood tall, scanning the room with an intense, focused purpose. She spotted Em laying on a lounge chair. "Stop!" she cried and ran forward. "Don't give her Shelby's blood."

Puentes and Martinez had moved to stand back-to-back protecting each other. They were tight, but flexed, ready to move as needed. Threatening.

Bobbie totally ignored them. She skirted around the ELLIS men and went straight to Em. Shelby still held out his arm and Dr. Mangot held a needle poised over it.

Bobbie gave Shelby's shoulder a small shove. "Go on. Help the others. I'm here." She sat and unzipped her wet suit and pulled it down, exposing a white bra. She held her left arm out toward Dr. Mangot while her eyes went to Em's face; her right hand slowly reached out to smooth a hair off Em's forehead.

She looked back at Dr. Mangot and nodded. "Get on with it."

Dr. Mangot nodded briskly and pulled out another alcohol swab. A moment later, blood started to flow into a plastic bag.

While Jake and the others watched the medical procedure play out, the ELLIS soldiers had raced wide toward the outer wall and were charging toward the doctor and her patient.

Dr. Mangot looked up sharply. "Look out!"

Jake shook himself like he was coming out of a trance. He scooted down a row of lounge chairs until he cut off their advance toward the doctor.

Puentes seemed happy to switch back to chasing Jake. He and Martinez raced between the lounge chairs trying to catch him.

With relief, Jake led them back toward the exit, away from the doctor. Once away, the four teens split into pairs. When Puentes jumped toward Jake and David, the boys went opposite directions forcing Puentes to choose which to chase after. If he went after Jake, David tossed a chair at him. If he spun around to go after David, Jake found a pile of towels and flung them at Puentes.

One landed draped over Puentes's head like a protection from the sun, blinding him for a second. Jake and David met up again and put more distance between themselves and the General.

Once David distracted Puentes, and Jake tried to swipe a cut at the officer. But this time, he couldn't cut through the wet suit. The knife glanced away and by then, Jake had to dodge back away to avoid Puente's reach.

Jillian and Shelby kept Martinez busy with similar tactics.

"How'd you find me?" asked Jake, panting. He needed to rest. If he could get the general talking, maybe they'd slow down.

The general snorted. "You remember that drink of tea you took on my boat? Full of nanobots."

"You've been tracking me!"

Puentes shrugged casually. "Just keeping an eye on my favorite alien. And now I've found your alien city, and we'll destroy it, too."

"You can't see what's right in front of you!" Jake couldn't believe the general was so dense. "Earth has always been different than you thought. The only difference now is that the Phoke have announced their presence to the world. Every hour, you see new video from a different Phoke city. There's a whole culture to discover there, a whole new 'world history' to be written. They've been hiding in plain sight for centuries."

"No." Puentes said flatly. "I'm not fooled by your propaganda. The Phoke are just Risonians in disguise. ELLIS will destroy this city. Today." He stopped chasing them and looked over his shoulder.

Jake sucked in a breath. "No!"

The teens had been chased around so much that Jake had lost track of where they were in the natatorium. General Puentes was positioned between Jake and the teens and Em's lounge chair.

Puentes turned and started toward Em.

Before the teens could do anything, Puentes had reached Dr. Mangot and shoved her roughly to the floor. He stood over Bobbie Fleming for a second before he put his knife under the tubing coming from her arm. He jerked it upward, and the soft tubing was cut clean in two. Blood spurted from the end still attached to Bobbie's arm. The blood bag—half full by now—drooped to the ground and blood oozed from the cut tubing.

Furious, Jake charged, followed by David, Jillian and Shelby. But Martinez was there, too, protecting the general's back.

Shelby shoved aside a chair and lunged, trying to tackle Martinez. Instead, Shelby slipped in the blood and his feet flew up. For a moment, he hung askew, and then his head hit the tile floor with a loud crack.

Unreasonably, Jake felt a pang of jealousy. Shelby was sacrificing himself for Em's sake. It should have been Jake who tried a diving tackle.

Jillian raced to Shelby and knelt to lean over him. "Are you okay?"

Shelby sat up and shook his head. "Maybe."

By now, Dr. Mangot was up. Calmly, she bent the tube still connected to Bobbie's arm to stop the blood flow. She put Bobbie's hand on it to keep it bent. And then, Dr. Mangot ignored everything but the blood bag. Quickly, she fitted a coupling into the cut end of the tubing. The coupling ran to a needle. She motioned for Bobbie to use her free hand to hold the bag up over Em's head while Dr. Mangot expertly slipped the needle into Em's vein.

Dr. Mangot turned her attention back to Bobbie, who was now contorted trying to keep the cut tube bent shut and still hold up Em's blood bag. Dr. Mangot pressed on the IV needle in Bobbie's arm and pulled it out, keeping a pressure on the arm. With her other hand, she grabbed a band aid from her case and pressed it to Bobbie's arm, and with relief, Fleming relaxed that hand.

Dr. Mangot looked at the blood bag and shook her head. "It's not enough. We need to do the other arm, now."

Bobbie's hair had started to dry, and curls spilled over into her face. She calmly blew them out of her eyes, changed hands holding up the blood bag, shifted on the lounge chair and offered Dr. Mangot her right arm.

While that was going on, the teens had moved as one toward Puentes. Shelby was up and moving, but slowly. Still, he was moving.

At Jake's nod, they rushed General Puentes. He might have fought off one, but their combined momentum carried everyone forward until they tumbled into the pool.

Jake held tight to Puentes's waist and pulled him deep. But Puentes was stronger, shoving him away and lashing out with kicks. Jake let him go, and with Velcroed legs kicked to the surface.

Looking around, David and Jillian had surfaced, too. Jake realized that while he wanted their help in fighting Puentes, absolutely, no way could anyone learn that they were Risonian.

"David, Jillian, you need to get out. I don't want you to drown."

They understood. Too much depended on making sure no one knew about the Risonian sleeper cells.

They kicked over to the side, but Martinez was there waiting. He'd found the knife that Jake had lost somehow in the melee, and threatened to use it. David kicked away from the wall and treaded water. But Jillian said practically, "Other side."

They quickly swam to the opposite side of the pool and pulled out. The deck there was narrow and not a strategic place to fight because of the danger of being forced into the pool. But that also made it a good retreat for Jillian and David.

Puentes had watched all this and yelled, "Martinez, you can shoot toward the pool."

"Ah," Martinez said.

He trained his pistol on Jake and pulled the trigger.

But Jake had already dived, ducking under the gunshot. Above, he saw Puentes's legs thrashing as he tried to reach the ladder. His equipment belt weighed him down, and he was tiring.

Warily, Jake surfaced with a quick look toward Martinez. He wasn't there. Jake scanned the pool's deck and there—

He dove!

Martinez had just moved around the pool to get a different angle on a shot.

A burning pain streaked across Jake's left shoulder. The bullet had grazed his left arm. A red stain spread in the water. He was bleeding.

Ironically, Jake thought, at least I'm not in the open ocean where the blood would call in sharks or something. He clamped his right hand over the wound to keep it from bleeding more.

Now it would be harder to keep Puentes in the water.

Suddenly, a tremendous wave hit him, and spinning around, he saw Shelby and Martinez grappling in the water. Shelby hit Martinez's hand, and the gun fell to the pool's floor. Shelby thrust Martinez deep into the pool, then turned and helped Jake to the side wall. Jillian and David helped heave him out.

Jake sat panting on the pool's edge.

David took over. "Each of us gets a side of the pool. Don't let them climb out."

Looking up, Jake realized that Puentes and Martinez were both still in the water.

"Jillian," David said, "Get their weapons."

Quickly, she handed a knife or gun to each teenager and they took up spots on the sides of the pool.

And it was a stand-off. Just like Earth and Rison were in a stand-off.

The natatorium was eerily quiet after all the echoing yells and fights.

Dr. Mangot called, "She's waking."

Jake wanted to rush to Em's side, but he had to keep the prisoners corralled.

The door slammed open yet again.

"Jake!"

It was Dad. Behind him were four men in Aberforth Hills militia uniforms.

Jake had never been so happy to see him.

"Here," he called.

Dad rushed to his side and at the sight of blood, his lips thinned in anger. "Are you OK?"

"It's minor," Jake said. "You shouldn't be here. You're supposed to be neutral."

Dad's eyes flared. He nodded toward the men in the pool. "And they shouldn't be here either."

Jake wanted to protest more because the U.S. Navy would court-martial Dad for disobeying the order. Especially if the press got wind that he was taking action instead remaining a neutral observer. But Jake was so relieved to see him.

"Let the doctor look at that." Dad's voice was rough with emotion. "Right now. That's an order."

Gratefully, Jake let other soldiers take his place and went to sit on the lounge chair beside Em.

Dr. Mangot tended his wound, pouring on antiseptic that stung, but Jake gently held Em's hand and never took his eyes off her.

She was too pale, but her eyes fluttered open now and then. Once, she squeezed his hand, and once, she whispered, "Jake."

Just to hear her say his name made Jake's heart swell with hope. She would live, and everything would be okay.

"You'll be fine," Dr. Mangot told Jake. "Just a shallow cut. It's long, but you'll be fine." She pointed to his hand. "Where'd you get that blister?"

"Jellyfish."

"What kind? What did it look like?" she demanded.

When he described it, Dr. Mangot whistled. "That was a Lion's Mane Jellyfish. It can kill a man." She stopped and tilted her head. "Do you need something on that blister?"

Jake lied, "No. It made a blister, but otherwise, I'm fine." No way was he telling her that it stopped his water breathing. No one must find out about that.

"It kills a man, but apparently barely bothers a Risonian. Interesting. I wonder—" she shook her head, as if to come back to the situation. She stood and called to the militia, "Commander Rose, are the corridors clear of ELLIS forces?"

"They pulled out," Dad said with a wide grin. "They can't really fight at this depth. They expected a small compound that they could come in and destroy with precision. Aberforth Hills surprised them."

"Then I need to get Em to the hospital. Now!" she said.

Dad strode to a storage closet and pulled out a collapsible cot. Jake wanted to help, but they wouldn't let him with his hurt shoulder. David, Jillian, and Shelby offered to help, but were waved off. In the end, Bobbie and a soldier picked up the cot and started to the door. Dr. Mangot followed with her medical case.

Jake hesitated. "Sir, do you need us?"

"Go," said Dad.

Nodding his thanks, Jake followed Em, along with David, Shelby, and Jillian.

RETREAT OF ELLIS

December 27, midday
By noon, the ELLIS attack had fallen back. All Puentes men had evacuated. Because their fancy new D-subs also doubled as decompression chambers, ELLIS forces could only operate easily for an hour before they had to decompress. But that also limited their attacks to about an hour. While decompressing, the soldiers had full access to control panels, so they could easily maneuver the sub and retreat from the area.

Dad had moved Puentes and Martinez to a locked room in Mangot Hospital, and then went to report to the Pentagon.

In their hurry to lock up the ELLIS men, though, they hadn't searched them. When the Aberforth Hillis militia unlocked the door to give a tray of food to each ELLIS soldier, they were ambushed. Puentes used tranquilizer darts to knock them out long enough for Puentes and Martinez to escape. The ELLIS men had hidden their deep-sea diving gear and apparently retrieved it.

Aberforth Hills hadn't had time, yet, to retrieve the unmanned subs that were floating near the city. Officials suspected Puentes found his submarine and escaped.

Bad weather still prevented satellite imagery or long-range radar for another day, and by then, everyone agreed that Puentes was long gone.

Jake wanted to celebrate. After all, they'd won! But he realizes the only reason for their victory was the ELLIS troop's restrictions on time spent at this depth. Their retreat was orderly and timely. They could come back, and next time, they'd know much more about Aberforth Hills. They might be able to target critical areas more easily.

ELLIS had inflicted a great deal of damage to the city. Three fourths of the city had been evacuated. Tunnel damage alone would cost millions, much less repair to buildings.

Phoke officials vowed that Aberforth Hills would rise again, bigger and better.

Meanwhile, the Battle of Aberforth Hills had broadcasted the brutality of the ELLIS Forces. The Phoke had won the publicity battle, with public opinion worldwide firmly on their side. Of course, the temptation of new tourist sites brought excitement, and the Water-Bed-and-Breakfast, or Water BNB, was flush with bookings, fueled by a steady stream of online videos.

The Phoke had come out in a most spectacular way.

COUSINS

December 31, New Year's Eve party

Lights flashed. Hung from the ceiling in the back room of the Bog Myrtle was an old-fashioned disco ball, a rotating ball of mirrors reflecting a dizzying glitter of light around the room. The Phoke Band was set up on the tiny stage and were belting out their particular brand of pulsing *nueva* folk music. Jake dodged around dancers, hands held high to protect the drinks he carried.

Em grinned up at him when he set the eggnog in front of her. They clinked glasses and Jake curiously took a sip. Hmmm. Sweet. It was a thick milky thing. Strange.

Em's eyebrows raised.

Jake shrugged, "It's OK."

Em was physically stronger, her complexion a healthier color. But it was nearing midnight and her eyes drooped. He wanted to dance with her, hold her close, but instead, they'd sat all night. Jake looked down the long table at Em's cousins who were chatting, eating, drinking and waiting for the new year to come in. This New Year's Eve party was thrown by Dr. Max especially to introduce Em to his three children. They lived in New Jack, the Phoke city in the Pacific Ocean near Seattle. Dr. Max's wife, Laxmi, was dark and beautiful.

When Dr. Max asked Em about the party, she had asked dubiously, "I have three cousins? And they're all three-fourths Phoke?"

"Yes," Dr. Max said. "Mindy, Juri and Konrad. When you go back to Seattle—which I hope isn't soon—you can visit them in New Jack."

At a nearby table, Mom and Dad visited with the adults. Mom was trying to take the night off from being an ambassador, but Jake saw that she was talking to the BBC announcer who had broadcast from Mangot Hospital during the Battle of Aberforth Hills. The gathered press would be leaving tomorrow, so this was one last chance for Mom to try to bend ears.

The lights flashed, the band crooned, and conversation ebbed and flowed. Jake sipped his eggnog, gazed around and thought about his last half year. He'd started Bainbridge High

School just five months ago, and shortly after he'd met Em. Fresh off the boat, as they say, he had just come to Earth from the moon base and knew nothing. He'd lived through the kidnapping of his mom and defeated a rogue ELLIS officer who had tried to sabotage Mt. Rainier with old Risonian technology. Now, he'd lived through the Battle of Aberforth Hills, an attack from another rogue ELLIS officer.

His biggest regret of the year was that Puentes had escaped and lived to fight another day. Captain Bulmer said that Puentes likely made it back to his submarine and escaped. He'd gone silent on his radar and no one knew where he was now.

Dr. Mangot's connections had worked quickly, and the Medical Mission to Rison would blast off in a week. Jake had to go up top tomorrow so they could fly out on the 2nd.

At first, they thought Bobbie Fleming would be going, but she'd had an announcement, too.

That morning, at Dr. Max's house, Jake and Em sat in the living room staring at Bobbie.

Obviously uncomfortable, she cleared her throat and said, "I'm not going back to Seattle."

"Why not?" Em asked.

"You know, when I talked with you that first time—"

Em nodded. "In the hospital, when you showed me the observation room."

"Yes," Bobbie nodded. "I was there for a procedure." She paused, looking up at the ceiling, avoiding Em's gaze.

"And?" asked Jake.

Her lips compressed, and she tucked a stray curl behind her ear. "Artificial insemination. I'm pregnant. It's from my eggs, so I'm the real mother."

"Oh," Em said. "A Phoke baby?" Her voice was soft, questioning.

"Yes."

Jake reached for Em's hand and squeezed it. Gently, he said, "A half sister or brother."

"Oh." Em was even more startled at that. "When?"

"August or September. So, I was wondering if you wanted to go to school here and maybe live with me this year?"

Em shook her head. "I'm going home. I'll have swim team and—" She paused, and then compressed her lips in a gesture so like her mother, and continued, "—I am Emmeline Tullis. My parents are Tullis. My sister is Tullis. I know now that I have a bigger family of Phoke and they are cool, too. I don't know how I'll fit in, but I'm willing to try to figure that out. But I also want to meet my biological father's family, too. I want to meet cousins on that side, too. I've already contacted them."

"Oh," said Bobbie. "Oh."

They stared at each other and finally Bobbie broke the silence. "Good," she said fiercely. "Be your own person. I'm glad that you've found Damien's family. You'll like them."

"Thanks for understanding," Em said with obvious relief. "I'll come and visit. If you'd like me to."

Bobbie smiled. "I'd like that."

Jake was glad they'd come to a sort of understanding. It would give Em the space she needed to learn who she was, and to learn more about her biological parents. She needed the time to come to terms with everything.

Bobbie's announcement meant the Medical Mission to Rison would include Dad, Jake, Captain Bulmer, and Dr. Mangot. What would the new year bring?

The countdown to midnight had started in earnest, with ten minutes left in the old year.

David leaned over Jake's chair and said, "Can we talk?"

Jake leaned toward Em and said, "I'll be right back."

He followed David to the back of the room where it was quiet enough to talk without yelling.

David said, "I don't know if I'll see you again till you get back, so I wanted to wish you an easy trip."

"Are you sad you're not coming?" If David didn't join the medical party, he'd never see Rison. By the time they got back, Rison would likely be gone.

"No, I'm an Earthling, through and through," David said. "But that's part of what I wanted to ask. This trip to Scotland, I've learned that I love politics. I'm a nobody, but it's been fun. Do you mind, could I ask your Mom if I could be her intern this summer?"

Jake remembered all the times David had been there with a calm word to prevent an argument. Back in Seattle, Jake had fallen into Puget Sound and should have been in hypothermia shock, but his magma-sapiens blood kept him warm and safe. David smoothed it over, hid Jake's alien nature, and convinced everyone that the unexpected swim in Puget Sound was nothing. At the diplomat's luncheon in Edinburgh, David smoothly talked to everyone while Jake had been nervous. When Captain Cook had argued about taking the *Gretchen* out to Aberforth Hills, David had cast it as just a tourist trip. Smooth. Calming. David was a natural diplomat.

"It's a perfect thing to do," Jake said earnestly. "Will you do it as a human or a Risonian?"

David's brow furrowed. "Don't know yet. But we'll work it out."

And Jake was sure he would.

"Five minutes!" shouted the crowd. It was almost midnight.

Jake worked his way back to Em's side.

"Four minutes!"

Jake and Em stood together under the disco ball lights and watched the countdown clock over the Phoke Band's heads.

Together, they shouted, "Three minutes!"

Jake didn't know what the next year would bring. The trip to Rison would be dangerous, and Em's health and permanent recovery was far from certain. But he was a different person than he had been on that far-away day on the Alabama beach when he'd gone swimming with the great white shark. Then, he had longed to know more about the Earth, and sometimes now, he thought he knew too much. But it was like Rison. Even though Rison was his home planet, he'd only seen a fraction of it. There was a lifetime to explore Earth.

"Two minutes!"

Em tugged on Jake's sleeve. "I'm tired," she yelled into his ear. She pulled him back to their table. She leaned back and closed her eyes.

"One minute!"

Reluctantly, Jake sat beside her and watched the crowd celebrate. When the countdown of seconds started, Em opened her eyes and weakly joined in. "Ten, nine, eight, seven, six, five, four, three, two, one."

The Phoke Band lit into a fast-paced Irish dance, and the dance floor was alive with people kissing, hugging and dancing. Em leaned back and closed her eyes again. With an aching heart, Jake held her hand and watched her quiet face.

BEFORE AND AFTER

January 1

The new year dawned on the North Sea with a brilliant blue sky. The winter storm had left a couple inches of snow, frozen water near the shore, and a crackling cold wind that caught at Jake's breath when he tried to speak. Yet he and Em walked the shore alone, the only place they could escape the chaos of everyone getting ready to travel. She couldn't go far, but they had to have one last good conversation.

The Risonians had rented the Coldingham Bay cottage again, and Em had been allowed to join them for a final goodbye breakfast. They had come up early this morning after the party at the Bog Myrtle. Em had taken a long nap and woke a bit stronger. When he suggested a short walk, she'd agreed.

Jake had to leave the next day for Florida to prepare for launch, and this was his last chance to talk to Em alone. His heart was so full and yet he found it hard to speak.

Instead, he held Em's hand as they walked, helping her climb over a patch of rocks to another clear space of beach. Her hoodie was tight around her face. Her cheeks were pink from the wind, her dark eyes glittering from the tears provoked by the wind. She was stronger today, but he had to remember not to push her too hard.

Finally they slowed and as if by mutual consent, they turned to gaze out at the North Sea. The waters were still tossed about and frothy. Ice crusted the quiet spots along the beach, but the surf kept other spots ice-free.

"Em, I'll miss you." He spoke calmly, though his insides were in turmoil.

"You don't have to go." Her voice held a plaintive hint. "It's not your fault, not your responsibility."

"That's where you're wrong," he said, speaking as much to himself as her. "I've been the Face of Rison because that's my duty. And it's always felt fake, like I was wearing a mask. This is different. I know what I have to do. This is my responsibility, what I was made to do. There are things that only I can do because I've been on Earth, and I know both worlds now. I swear to you, I'll bring back a cure for the *umjaadi*."

Her dark eyes were fixed on his face. "Yes, I see that. This is you. But I don't want you to go if you are just feeling guilty. Because it's not your fault. The *umjaadi* was an accident. It's a fluke that I was the first to get sick from it."

For a moment, Jake let himself get lost in those eyes. But time was short. "Partly, I feel guilty, yes," he said. "But I'm also worried that if I don't go, my step-father won't evacuate and leave Rison. Humans have a saying for it: the captain goes down with his ship. But that's stupid."

She turned to him and squeezed his hand. "Don't be stupid, either. Don't go down with the ship."

Jake turned to her, too, and nodded. He pulled a small gift box from his jacket. "I have something for you."

The box was no bigger than her fist. Quickly, she tore open the paper. Jake held out his hand, and when she handed it to him, he stuffed the paper into his pocket.

She lifted the lid and gasped. "Amber?"

Jake grinned and fastened the golden mermaid around her neck. "Don't take it off till I get home," he said. "I'll be back. I promise."

"Is that a promise you can keep?"

Jake stared at her dark lashes that blinked back tears. Her face was a dark golden color like the amber mermaid, the rich color of her Japanese father. Underneath there was still a pallor from the *umjaadi* illness, and the dark hoodie made her face even more stark. But she was his siren, his call from the Earth's sea.

He dipped his head, and finally—there was no one to stop the kiss.

But the kiss stopped Jake's world. Soft, electric, breathtaking. It was as if he'd been living in space, in a vacuum, but it was no longer empty because Em filled up all the dark emptiness.

This is a turning point in my life, he thought. *It will always be before the kiss and after the kiss.*

He hoped there would be many more kisses. But this one? It changed everything. His heart swelled and he dared name the emotion: love. He vowed that he would be back for more, and he would bring her a cure.

SIRENS

Jake held her hand close to his heart, and Em's head rested on his chest where she surely heard his heart thumping in a wild joy.

Em was his siren; and he was hers. One day, together, they would explore all the seas of the planet called Earth.

BLAST OFF

January 7

The Kennedy Space Center at Cape Canaveral, Florida, was crowded with spectators.

Commercial vehicles traveled to and from the Moon Base making it a bustling port-of-entry. But the medical mission would launch from the interstellar platform that had been built in the last ten years to accommodate Risonian ships.

Mom had come to see Dad and Jake off. From his backpack, Jake pulled out a small gift-wrapped package.

"Mom, this is your birthday present. I'm sorry it's a couple days late."

"Oh, thank you."

She pulled the ribbon to untie it and ripped open the paper. Opening the jeweler's box, the amber mermaid gleamed against the black velvet. Mom's eye widened and she cried out with surprise. "So beautiful."

Jake shrugged. "I bought it at the Aberforth Jewelers in Edinburgh before we found out anything about Aberforth Hills. But I hoped you'd still like it."

Mom turned and let Dad fasten the necklace around her neck. Touching the mermaid, she said, "I won't take it off till you return." Her voice choked. "Come back, you hear me, come back."

Jake nodded. "I will. I'll try to bring Swann with me."

A sudden homesickness swept over him. How he'd missed Rison! But when he'd left, he was a child. Would Swann accept him as older and wiser, or still treat him like a child? Would he still be proud of Jake? Would he still love Jake?

Mom turned and buried her face in Dad's shoulder. They hugged tight for a moment, and then she pushed gently away. The odd Risonian wrinkle on her forehead and nose deepened, the only sign that she was having trouble holding back her emotions.

Dr. Mangot called, "It's time to board."

The Medical Mission to Rison was ready. Dad and Jake led the way, followed by the Phoke pair, Dr. Mangot and Captain

Bulmer. Mom, David, and Jillian had linked arms, as if they needed support to watch loved ones blast off toward danger.

The news reports were full of suspicions: There were fears that Jake Quad-de was returning home with intelligence that would allow the Risonians to attack. His mother, Ambassador Dayexi Quad-de assured the press that he only returned to bring back a cure for the Phoke. But no one was quite sure why Jake would risk his life for the Phoke. Equally feared was that Dr. Mangot was a Phoke ambassador who would negotiate a treaty of water people versus the land people. Until they returned, David, Mom and the rest of the sleepers would have public relations work to do.

Once on board, Jake and Dad made their way to the viewing port and strapped into seats where they could watch the crowd as they launched. The latest spaceships lacked the drama of twentieth century launches with their huge blasts of fire. Instead the newest propulsion systems, based on Risonian technology, were quiet and efficient, sending them hurtling toward space.

Jake had lived on the Obama Moon Base for about eighteen months and watched Earth's blue oceans circle and circle them. Earth-rise and Earth-set. But this time, at the sight of the blue planet, home-sickness swept over him. He was Risonian born, but his Earth blood drew him to this small blue planet as surely as flowers heavy with pollen draws bees.

Earth filled the viewport for the first hour, but soon, it grew smaller and smaller, until it was a blue ball hanging in the black of space. His planet. Yes, it was his planet now. But to save his planet, there was work to be done on Rison.

Jake turned his face toward Rison and the Turco star system and hoped.

The End

Join Jake in *Book 3*,
The Blue Planets World series,
PILGRIMS

ABOUT THE AUTHOR

Translated into nine languages, children's book author
DARCY PATTISON writes picture books, middle grade nov-
els, and children's nonfiction. Her work has been recognized
by *starred reviews* in *Kirkus*, *BCCB*, and *PW*. Three books
have been named National Science Teachers Association Out-
standing Science Trade Books: *Desert Baths* (2013); *Abayomi, the
Brazilian Puma* (2015), and *Nefertiti, the Spidernaut* (2017). *The
Nantucket Sea Monster: A Fake News Story* is a Fall 2017 Junior
Library Guild selection. She is a member of the Society of
Children's Bookwriters and Illustrators and the Author's
Guild. For more information, see
darcypattison.com/about OR mimshouse.com

Join our mailing list:
MimsHouse.com/newsletter/

OTHER NOVELS BY DARCY PATTISON
Saucy and Bubba: A Hansel and Gretel Tale
The Girl, the Gypsy and the Gargyole
Vagabonds
Liberty
Longing for Normal

The Aliens, Inc. Series – short chapter books
Book 1: Kell, the Alien
Book 2: Kell and the Horse Apple Parade
Book 3: Kell and the Giants
Book 4: Kell and the Detectives

DARCY PATTISON

SIRENS

DARCY PATTISON

SIRENS